W9-COY-555

Through the window, Wishbone saw the top of a small oak tree move across his view of the front yard.

"A walking tree?" Surprised and excited, Wishbone rolled over, forgetting for the moment that he was lying at the edge of his big red chair. "Whoa! Hey!"

The white-with-black-and-brown-spots dog hit the floor with a small *thud*.

"Who? What? Where?" Wishbone quickly jumped to his feet and looked back to the window. The last of the treetop disappeared from his view. "Hey! No tree walks out of my yard!" He took off into the kitchen and ran outside through his doggie door.

Wishbone trotted across the backyard. He could have moved much faster, but he needed time to think about what he had just seen.

"Okay, Wishbone," he said to himself, "you've just seen a tree walk across your front lawn. What is the meaning of this?" Wishbone trotted past a couple of bikes that were lying on the ground. "Trees are supposed to have roots, not legs!" The terrier rounded a corner of the house and headed into the side yard. "But what if some trees have suddenly grown legs?" He hopped over a coiled garden hose. "What if they're trying to walk away?" He was almost to the front yard. "Where will I be if they all take off?"

The Adventures of WISHBONE™ titles in Large-Print Editions:

The Adventures of WISHBONE™

DIGGING TO THE CENTER OF THE EARTH

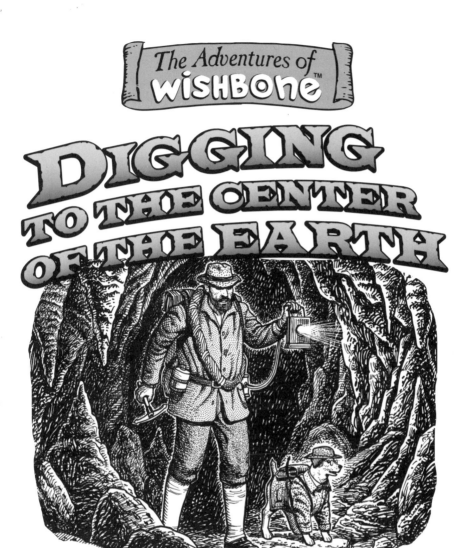

by Michael Anthony Steele
Based on the teleplay by Jack Wesley
Inspired by *A Journey to the Center of the Earth*
by Jules Verne

WISHBONE™ created by Rick Duffield

Gareth Stevens Publishing
MILWAUKEE

For a free color catalog describing Gareth Stevens' list of high-quality books and multimedia programs, call 1-800-542-2595 (USA) or 1-800-461-9120 (Canada). Gareth Stevens Publishing's Fax: (414) 225-0377.

Library of Congress Cataloging-in-Publication Data

Steele, Michael Anthony.
    Digging to the center of the earth / by Michael Anthony Steele; [interior illustrations by Don Punchatz].
        p. cm.
    Originally published: Allen, Texas; Big Red Chair Books, © 1999.
    (The adventures of Wishbone; #17)
        Summary: When he uncovers a mysterious metal object while digging in the front yard, Wishbone imagines himself as Professor Otto Lidenbrock who attempts to discover the center of the earth by leading an expedition into the crater of an Icelandic volcano.
        ISBN 0-8368-2595-0 (lib. bdg.)
        [1. Science fiction. 2. Dogs—Fiction.] I. Punchatz, Don, ill. II. Verne, Jules, 1828-1905. Journey to the center of the earth. III. Title. IV. Adventures of Wishbone; #17.
    PZ7.S8147Di   2000
    [Fic]—dc21   99-051790

This edition first published in 2000 by
Gareth Stevens Publishing
1555 North RiverCenter Drive, Suite 201
Milwaukee, Wisconsin 53212 USA

© 1999 Big Feats! Entertainment. First published by Big Red Chair Books™, a Division of Lyrick Publishing™, 300 E. Bethany Drive, Allen, Texas 75002.

Edited by Kevin Ryan
Continuity editing by Grace Gantt
Copy edited by Jonathon Brodman
Cover design by Lyle Miller
Interior illustrations by Don Punchatz
Wishbone photograph by Carol Kaelson

1 2 3 4 5 6 7 8 9 04 03 02 01 00

For Anne Power,
who fashioned me from clay

FROM THE BIG RED CHAIR . . .

Oh . . . hi! Wishbone here. You caught me right in the middle of some of my favorite things—books. Let me welcome you to THE ADVENTURES OF WISHBONE. In each of these books, I have adventures with my friends in Oakdale and imagine myself as a character in one of the greatest stories of all time. This story takes place in the spring, when Joe is twelve, and he and his friends are in the sixth grade—during the first season of my television show.

In *DIGGING TO THE CENTER OF THE EARTH*, I imagine I'm Professor Otto Lidenbrock, a scientist from Jules Verne's *A JOURNEY TO THE CENTER OF THE EARTH*. It's an exciting adventure about a determined professor whose fantastic voyage far beneath the Earth's surface allows him to discover more than he ever imagined!

You're in for a real treat, so pull up a chair and a snack and sink your teeth into *DIGGING TO THE CENTER OF THE EARTH!*

Chapter One

"One hundred twenty-two . . . one hundred twenty-three . . . and one hundred twenty-four." Wishbone finished counting as he lay sprawled across the seat of a living room chair. The terrier's brown-and-white-spotted ears pointed down at the floor as his head hung lazily over the edge. "In case anyone wants to know," he announced to the Talbot house, "there are exactly one hundred twenty-four tiles covering our living room ceiling."

Wishbone sighed.

"So . . . this is what it means to be bored."

It was a lazy Saturday afternoon in Oakdale, and Wishbone was very, very, extremely, incredibly bored. He had counted all of the living room ceiling tiles. He had buried everything he owned—twice! He had even checked the house several times for intruders. Wishbone had thought about taking a nap, but he was even too bored to sleep.

"Let's see," the dog said, rolling over. "First, I was bored in the study. Then I was bored in the backyard. I was bored in the kitchen, *if you can believe that*. Then I was bored here in the living room." He changed his position again. "What a day. This bored dog has been bored in every part of the entire boring house." Wishbone rolled onto his back. "Maybe I should go back into the study. It was a little less boring in there. Plus, I think I only counted the ceiling tiles three times in there."

Suddenly, Wishbone jumped to his feet on the chair.

"Wait a minute!" he said, his head cocked to one side. "What if this is it? What if I've already done every-thing there is to do?"

He jumped down onto the living room floor and began to walk back and forth. "What if I've been on all of the adventures I can go on?" He circled left. "What if I've eaten all of the treats there are to eat?" He circled right. "What if there's nothing left for me to do in the whole . . . wide . . . world!" He took two quick steps, leaped into the air, and spun completely around. *"Aaaaaaaahhhhhhhh!"*

Wishbone quickly jumped back onto the chair.

"Heh-heh!" he laughed. "There's nothing like a little full-blown panic to cure a case of boredom." He turned a circle on the chair's cushion, then plopped back down. "Well, that was fun," the dog said with a yawn and a wag of his tail. "But what I really need is some genuine, nose-sniffin', tail-waggin' excitement!" He rolled over and looked out the front window. He yawned again. "I know—maybe I can count the leaves on that walking tree."

Through the window, Wishbone saw the top of a small oak tree move across his view of the front yard.

"A walking tree?" Surprised and excited, Wishbone rolled over, forgetting for the moment that he was lying on the edge of the chair. "Whoa! Hey!"

The white-with-brown-and-black-spots dog hit the floor with a small *thud*.

"Who? What? Where?" Wishbone quickly jumped to his feet and looked back to the window. The last of the treetop disappeared from his view. "Hey! No tree walks out of my yard!" He took off into the kitchen and ran outside through his doggie door.

Wishbone trotted across the backyard. He could have moved much faster, but he needed time to think about what he had just seen.

"Okay, Wishbone," he said to himself, "you've just seen a tree walk across your front lawn. What is the meaning of this?" Wishbone trotted past a couple of bikes that were lying on the ground. "Trees are supposed to have roots, not legs!" The terrier rounded a corner of the house and headed into the side yard. "But what if some trees have suddenly grown legs?" He hopped over a coiled garden hose. "What if they're trying to walk away?" He was almost to the front yard. "Where will I be if they all take off?"

As Wishbone trotted around the corner to the front yard, he came face-to-wheel with Wanda Gilmore's brightly colored wheelbarrow. And that wheelbarrow was about to flatten the cute little dog!

"Ahhh! Look out!" Wishbone yelled as he jumped to the side. He narrowly escaped being run over by the bright green-and-yellow, yet nicely painted, wheelbarrow.

"Whoa! Wishbone! Watch out!" Wanda cried, pulling back on the two yellow handles.

Wanda Gilmore was the next-door neighbor of Wishbone and the Talbot family. Although she was a bit unusual, the thin, auburn-haired lady was always a kind and caring friend—unless, of course, you happened to get caught burying most of your worldly possessions in her yard. Unfortunately, because her yard had the best digging dirt in all of Oakdale, Wishbone wasn't always on Wanda's good side. She could never stay angry with him for long, though. After Wishbone would do his digging and get a scolding, life would soon return to normal—

that is, until the next time. There was always one thing that you could count on with Wanda Gilmore—life definitely perked up when she was around.

Wishbone gazed up at Wanda. She was dressed in a T-shirt with a brightly colored workshirt over it, slacks, and gardening gloves. It was clear that Wanda was dressed for dirt. The dog's eyes quickly moved from Wanda to the items that were in her wheelbarrow. There was a shovel, a water cooler, and . . . a small oak tree!

"You've caught the walking tree!" Wishbone said with relief. "Good job, Wanda!" He was also relieved to see that the tree's roots were surrounded by a burlap bag full of dirt. That was good. No legs there.

Joe Talbot, Wishbone's twelve-year-old roommate and best friend, stepped off their front porch. "Wishbone, watch where you're going," he said as he came toward the little traffic jam.

"Sorry, Joe, I'm just making sure all trees are present and accounted for!" Wishbone gave a look back to the tree just to make sure.

From around the other corner of the house came Joe's friends Samantha Kepler and David Barnes. They were both very special friends to Joe and Wishbone. David, a kid who could build almost anything out of all sorts of odds and ends, had the curiosity and the interest in gaining knowledge that Wishbone always admired in a human. And Samantha—or "Sam," for short—was the kind of caring friend who was always there to support others. Her adventurous spirit was also something Wishbone admired. Put those two kids together with Joe Talbot, and a dog couldn't ask to be part of a better pack.

"Hi, Joe. Hi, Miss Gilmore," David and Sam said as they walked up to the group. Sam kneeled and began to scratch Wishbone behind the ears. "How's your day going, Wishbone?" she asked.

"Sam, it's a long story," he replied, one of his hind legs beginning to kick from pleasure. "But if you keep scratching, I'll be happy to tell you all about it."

"Hi," Joe said to Sam and David. He then turned back to Wanda. She seemed to be struggling with her tree-filled wheelbarrow. "Miss Gilmore, do you need a hand?" the brown-haired boy asked.

"No . . . no . . . I've got it," Wanda replied, still struggling. "I'm okay." The tree wobbled back and forth in her wheelbarrow. She kept the same motion going by moving her wheelbarrow back and forth, as well. Wishbone thought it was quite a sight. Then, suddenly, the tree got the better of her. It began to lean far out of the wheelbarrow. It was clearly out of control.

Wishbone jumped back. "Hey, Wanda, don't let it get away!"

The kids ran over and grabbed the trunk of the tree. They kept it from toppling to the ground. Wanda lowered the two yellow handles, letting the wheelbarrow rest on its two support legs. "Well, you know, maybe I *do* need a little help," she said. She wiped her brow with the back of a gloved hand. "Here, you kids push the wheelbarrow. I'll find the right spot for the tree."

"Good idea!" Wishbone barked in agreement. "Let's get that thing back in the ground, where it belongs!"

The kids took charge of the wheelbarrow. Joe held one handle, while David grabbed the other. Sam steadied the tree's thin trunk. She held it in such a way that it couldn't take another plunge. They followed Wanda as she wandered around Joe's front yard, looking for just the right spot. Wishbone cautiously kept his distance.

"Well, this looks like the perfect spot right here," Wanda said, satisfied with the particular patch of yard she had chosen. "Okay, kids, bring it over here." But just as the kids wheeled the tree over, Wanda walked to

11

another part of the yard. "You know, if we put it over here, then it'll get the sun from that direction." Wanda turned to the kids, just as they set down their heavy load. "Okay, you three, let's set it right here, all right?"

The kids, once again, lifted the awkward wheelbarrow and its contents. They shakily wheeled it over to where Wanda now stood. They plopped it down with a huge sigh of relief. Seeing that the danger was over, Wishbone also walked over to Wanda.

"Wanda, what exactly are you doing?" he asked.

Sam let go of the tree. "What exactly are you doing, Miss Gilmore?" she repeated, unknowingly.

Wishbone turned to Sam. "Sam, you read my mind."

"Well, you may not know it, but today is . . ." Wanda finished her thought by pulling open her brightly colored top shirt, revealing her T-shirt underneath. On the T-shirt, two large printed words rested under a picture of an oak tree.

"Arbor Day?" Joe asked, reading the words on the shirt.

"That's the day when we celebrate trees," Sam said.

Wishbone sat up on his haunches. "For your information, I celebrate trees *every* day!"

Wanda turned to Joe. "It's the day when we remember how important trees are to us." She looked around to the others. "They provide shade and beauty and produce oxygen for us to breathe. Every year, on Arbor Day, I plant a tree." She motioned to her tree-filled front yard. "And this year, I said to myself, 'Wanda, why don't you be a good neighbor and share your joy with someone else?' And so I decided to plant a tree for you and your mom, Joe." Joe smiled as she continued. "But I guess I could be convinced to let you guys help."

The kids looked at one another. Sam and David

swapped a quick glance and a smile. Sam said, "Well, okay, Miss Gilmore."

"That's the spirit!" Wanda said excitedly, reaching into her wheelbarrow.

Joe looked around. "So, where do we start?" he asked.

Wanda pulled out the shovel. "Well, you dig, of course." She handed the tool to Joe. "I've got a few more shovels in my backyard. I'll go get them and be back in a jiffy." She started to leave, then turned back to the kids. "Oh, there's some water there in case you get thirsty." Then she took off toward her house.

"Did someone say 'dig'?" Wishbone barked eagerly, and his ears perked up. "This is going to be great!" He watched Joe begin to dig the hole. "Joe, you start, while I keep an eye on the tree." Wishbone walked up to the tree. "I've got some plans for you, tree, heh-heh!"

Everyone watched as Joe pulled the dirt-filled shovel from the ground. He dumped its contents into a neat pile beside the newly formed hole.

Wishbone's attention was drawn from the tree to the pile of dirt. He took in a deep breath. "Ah, the smell of fresh dirt in the afternoon." He pawed at some of the fresh chunks. "Joe, you're doing a topnotch job. Just look at this big piece!" he said, his tail wagging with happiness.

Wishbone's tail continued to wag.

"You know, Joe, your digging is really great." Wishbone's paws tightened. "But maybe you could use a break." His tail wagging even faster, Wishbone could hardly control his excitement. "Uh . . . Joe?" Wishbone watched as Joe kept digging, the lovely smell of the fresh earth drifting Wishbone's way with every stroke of the shovel. Why should Joe be able to keep all the fun to himself?

That's it! Wishbone thought. He could stand no more! The dog dove, headfirst, into the hole!

"My turn!" he yelled, as dirt began to fly under his paws.

As the soil came loose from the earth, Wishbone's happiness grew with every pawful. Digging was definitely his most favorite thing to do in the whole wide world . . . well, except for eating. Okay, it was one of his two most favorite things to do . . . well, except for chasing cats. All right—eating, digging, chasing cats . . . oh, and don't forget books! Okay, okay—"all of the above" were on Wishbone's list of favorite things to do in the whole wide world. And since there wasn't a cat, book, or ginger snap in sight, digging won for now.

He dug deeper and deeper, faster and faster. Even through the sound of his nails tearing into the earth and the dirt flying past his hind legs, Wishbone was able to hear the kids exclaim with amazement about the amount of dirt he was moving. More important, he could hear Joe's reply.

"He's a digging machine," Joe said to his friends.

Wishbone's heart soared, knowing he was making his boy proud. He must dig harder and faster!

But, just as he was going into doggie-overdrive, he felt something hard beneath his nails. It wasn't as hard as a rock, but it was not your average dirt clod.

Wishbone carefully cleaned away the dirt from around the object. Then he reached down and grabbed the round, flat item with his mouth. It was about three inches in diameter. "Nope, it definitely doesn't taste like a rock," he said, as he jumped out of the hole.

"Whatcha got there, boy?" Joe asked, seeing the dirt-covered object in the dirt-covered dog's mouth.

"I just dig the stuff up, pal. I don't analyze it," the dirty terrier replied as he turned toward Joe. "But I do

know it's not a rock. Rocks have a more . . . well . . . rocky taste."

Joe reached down and removed the object from Wishbone's mouth. He turned it over in his hand. "Oh, it's just an old piece of junk," he said, handing it to David.

Wishbone spat bits of dirt out of his mouth. "It tasted old, too."

Sam came close as David looked down and examined the disk. "I don't think this is just a piece of junk," he said, trying to scrape away the rest of the dirt. As some of it fell away, a pale yellow color was revealed.

Sam pointed to something near the edge of the piece. "Hey, it looks like there's writing on it," she said.

David quickly began to remove the dirt from around the spot where Sam was pointing. "Yeah, I see. It looks like initials." He scraped some more dried soil away with his fingernail. "It looks like the letters . . . N. J." David looked up at his friends. "This could be something really important!"

"Well, there's only one way to find out," Joe said. "Let's take it inside and clean it up!"

Wishbone watched as the kids ran toward the

house. Wanda came around the corner just as they reached the front steps.

"Hey, where is everybody going? Who is going to help?" she asked.

Wishbone went back to the freshly dug hole and peered inside. "Hmm . . . mysterious initials on an ancient artifact. That sounds very familiar." He let his imagination take over. The hole seemed much deeper and wider now. It seemed deep enough to plant a hundred trees inside—maybe even a thousand! His imagination carried him further. Now the hole was so deep that it seemed to stretch to the very center of the Earth itself!

Wishbone's head snapped up, and he came out of his daydream. "That's it!" he shouted. "That's what that mysterious artifact reminds me of! This is just how Professor Lidenbrock's adventure began in Jules Verne's classic novel, *A Journey to the Center of the Earth!*"

A Journey to the Center of the Earth is a classic science-fiction novel. And *science* fiction is one of my favorite kinds of fiction. It's the kind of story in which incredible things can happen, but they are still very believable because they're based on real scientific facts or ideas. And this fantastic story is no exception!

What if you were able to travel very, very, very deep down inside the Earth? What would it be like? And what would you find once you were there? Well, those were the questions Jules Verne answered when he wrote *A Journey to the Center of the Earth.*

The story takes place in 1863, and it begins in the

city of Hamburg, Germany. Professor Otto Lidenbrock, a well-educated man who teaches and studies the science of geology, and his nephew, Axel, are about to find a mysterious artifact. This will lead them on the most fantastic adventure of their lives!

Chapter Two

Wishbone sat next to the fresh mound of dirt and peered, once again, into the freshly-dug hole. He imagined himself to be the very well educated Professor Lidenbrock, running down a village road, on his way home with something very special.

Tail wagging, Professor Lidenbrock trotted through the seaport village of Hamburg. The little town was full of all the sights and sounds of transatlantic ocean trade. Sea gulls shrieked overhead as cargo was loaded onto and off the many tall ships safely anchored in the harbor.

But all of this activity was shut out of the professor's mind. On this day, May 24, 1863, his mind was focused only on returning home. The brisk, salt air chilled his whiskers, but he kept up his quick pace. People he knew greeted him as he passed, but he kept on going. The cobblestones of the street were hard against his soft paws, but he paid little attention to the ground underneath him. It seemed that the professor couldn't get home fast enough. For, in his mouth, he held a most incredible discovery. His teeth gently grasped an aged and yellowing book.

The professor loved to collect old books. Although this one probably held little value to anyone else, it was especially important to him. It was from Iceland—an island country in the far north Atlantic Ocean whose culture and history were one of the professor's favorite topics of study. Even more important, the book was written in runes, the original letters of the language of Iceland! Runes were used for writing between the fourth and fourteenth centuries.

Professor Lidenbrock knew that the book must tell of some treasure, some unknown fact, or some important data that only he would be able to decode from the ancient text. Although he spoke many languages, Icelandic was not one of them. He couldn't wait to get home and begin translating it. He knew that his nephew, Axel, would not be as thrilled over this remarkable find as he was. Still, he couldn't wait to show it to him.

Professor Lidenbrock cared deeply for Axel. The young man had been living with the professor and studying under his guidance for some time now. The professor was beginning to realize that Axel was an excellent student, as well as a fine scientist in his own right. The professor was also very much pleased that his nephew's passion lay in the same field of science that he himself so loved—geology, the study of the development of the different layers of the Earth's crust.

Although Axel wasn't always as enthusiastic about the subject as Lidenbrock was, the professor still encouraged his nephew's thirst for knowledge. He also involved his nephew in everything that he did. Professor Lidenbrock saw a young version of himself every time he looked at Axel.

The professor arrived at his front gate. He trotted through the always-open entryway to his yard. It was always open because the gate hung awkwardly by only one hinge. It had been like that for many years, with no hope of repair. Who had time to repair a gate when there were great scientific discoveries to make, and unusual rock specimens to study and label?

The professor trotted up the front walk. He went past the grand oak tree that stood in the front yard. He proceeded up to the ivy-covered cottage that was his and his nephew's home. Upon reaching the front door, he pushed it open with his front paws. The professor entered the house, tail wagging with excitement.

"Ac-thul! Ac-thul! Dear boy!" he called with a bit of difficulty, the old book still in his mouth. "Ac-thul, come here at onth!"

The professor ran up the stairs toward his study. As he climbed the stairs, he heard, from the dining room, the clink of silverware against porcelain, then the clomping footsteps of his nephew. *I must have interrupted Axel's dinner,* the professor thought, as he walked through the study's doorway. *No matter, he must come and see this incredible book!*

Professor Lidenbrock shook off his hat and hopped onto a chair next to a table. The table was littered with all the necessary tools of the serious geologist: books, various picks, mallets, and magnifying glasses. And rocks—there were plenty of rocks, all in various stages of being tested, labeled, and classified.

As he brushed aside some of the clutter with his paws, dust filled the air. All the tiny particles were immediately spotlighted by the warm rays of the setting sun. The amber light shone through the window and onto the museum of cataloged specimens that made up the professor's study.

He set down the ancient book and adjusted his spectacles. Then, quickly, but carefully, he leafed through it. "Wonderful!" he cried, his paw turning another page. "Wonderful! Wonderful!"

Axel stepped into the study and came over to the table. He was clearly curious about the cause for such a commotion. "What have you found, Uncle?" he asked.

He looked up at his tall, nice-looking nephew. A napkin still tucked into his shirt collar proved the professor's theory of the unfinished dinner downstairs.

"Axel, my boy," the professor replied, "this book is a true and correct account of the Norwegian people who settled the island of Iceland. I'm sure it will give us some never-before-revealed information on the subject!"

Axel showed a small bit of enthusiasm, but Professor Lidenbrock knew his nephew was just trying to make him happy. "Wonderful, Uncle," Axel said. "The volume is translated into German, I hope."

"Absolutely not," his uncle replied, a bit annoyed by the idea. "I wouldn't pay a penny for a plain old translation." He turned another page. "This is in the Icelandic language, written in runes. That is what makes the book so valuable to me! More often than not, bad translations change many of the names and confuse the facts!" He motioned with his nose for Axel to take a closer look.

Axel reached over and picked up the open book. When he turned it around to look at it more closely, a small scrap of paper fell to the table. "It's so old, it's falling apart, Uncle," Axel said jokingly.

But the professor didn't think this remark was a joke. He seized the small scrap in his mouth, before it hit the table. He set it down in front of him and looked it over.

"No, Axel, it seems that this piece of parchment is not as old as the book itself. But the writing on it is also in runes."

21

The small scrap measured about five by three inches. Professor Lidenbrock examined it carefully. He suddenly became more excited.

"Axel!" he cried. "I believe this note must have been written by the previous owner of this text. Quickly! Search through the manuscript!" the professor said, his tail wagging excitedly. "Perhaps, by great good luck, the person's name will be written somewhere inside the volume!"

Axel picked up a magnifying glass and began to flip through the pages of the ancient book. His search was brief. "Here, Uncle." He turned the book around and pointed to a faded, almost unreadable inscription, written on the fly leaf—the blank sheet at the beginning of the book.

With the professor's keen eyesight, he made out the name. "Arne Saknussemm . . . Arne Saknussemm!" he cried in a joyous and thrilled tone. "That is not only an Icelandic name, but the name of a very wise professor of the sixteenth century!" The professor's tail wagged quickly. "Arne Saknussemm was a famous scientist who made several important discoveries while looking for ways to change metals—such as mercury or lead—into gold!" He leaped to the floor and bowed deeply in respect for the great scientist.

He then rose and walked around the study, his tail still wagging. He couldn't believe what a great treasure he had found.

"Axel, if this note has truly been written by the great Saknussemm himself, then I'm sure it must have some very important secret meaning!" He hopped back up onto the stool. "We must try to translate and decode it!" He looked at the parchment once more.

"You may be right, Uncle," Axel said with a bit of hesitation, "but what is the point of keeping it a secret from future generations, especially if it tells of a useful and worthy discovery?"

Professor Lidenbrock looked at his nephew. "How should I know? Didn't the great scientist Galileo keep secret his discovery of the rings of Saturn, for fear of being punished by the authorities?" He returned his attention to the scrap of paper. "Until I discover the meaning of this note, I will neither eat nor sleep!"

Axel stared at his uncle in surprise. "You, Uncle? Not eat?" he said, referring to his uncle's normally huge appetite.

The professor thought to himself, *Did I say no eating?* "Well," he said, looking directly at Axel, "maybe a little snack wouldn't hurt." His thoughts then turned back to the mysterious note. "What am I saying?" Ignoring his growling stomach, Professor Lidenbrock turned back to the small piece of parchment. "No, I meant what I said—until this mystery is solved, no food or sleep for me."

Well into the night, the professor and Axel puzzled over the strange message. The pair started out to do what they thought would be the simple job of translating Icelandic into German. However, the task turned out to be something of a brain-teaser. Once Professor Lidenbrock had translated the text, letter-for-letter, word-for-word, only gibberish remained.

The two tested several different ways of solving the puzzle. They tried grouping the letters together by twos, then by threes, then by fours and fives. They had no success at all. The professor pawed through a few dictionaries of several different languages, but that was no help, either. It seemed this was an unbreakable code.

Eventually, the warm light of the sunrise began to pour into the study. The professor jumped down from his stool and began to walk back and forth. He was deep in thought. There had to be an answer to this frustrating puzzle. No matter how long it took, he would not rest until the parchment gave up its secret. No matter how many combinations and methods he had to use, the professor knew he would find the correct one!

As he walked, he saw Axel lean back in his chair, frustrated and tired. "Maybe it's time for a break," the professor said to Axel to comfort him. He stopped moving so he could rub his aching eyes. His growling stomach was also telling him it was time for food.

When the professor felt some relief in his eyes, he looked back at Axel. He was fanning himself with the secretive piece of parchment. The professor watched as the note swayed back and forth.

He saw the front of the paper, then the back; the front, then the back.

The light from the lamp on the table lit the paper from behind as it waved in Axel's hand.

Front . . . back.

The sheet wasn't very thick, so the letters could be seen clearly from the back of the page, when some light was behind it.

Front . . . back.

Staring lazily at the floating page, Professor Lidenbrock noticed something. He was sure he could make some sense out of all the jumbled letters. Although they were backward from where he stood, the order they were in seemed to form words he could understand. He made out the word *descend*.

Front . . .

Back . . .

Then he recognized the words *crater* and *Sneffels*.

Front . . .

Back . . .

Back? . . .

The fur on the professor's neck stood up. Back! That was it! It was so simple, but yet so very difficult to put a paw on!

"I have discovered the secret!" the professor cried out, his tail wagging wildly.

"What is it, Uncle?" Axel asked, as he seemed to be pulled from a daydream.

Professor Lidenbrock leaped back onto his stool. "Axel, dear boy, hold the parchment up to the lamp with the blank side facing you."

Axel did as his uncle told him to, and his eyes widened.

"Do you see, Axel?" the professor said with excitement. He stared at the parchment.

"Yes, Uncle," Axel replied. "The message is beginning to make sense now. You have to read the note . . . backward!"

A feeling of complete success washed over the professor's soul. He felt as if he had found the cure for all diseases! He felt as if he had just reached the top of the highest mountain on the planet! There lay the answer, simple as it was, right before his eyes. It was as if Saknussemm's ghost had pointed it out himself!

"Oh, most clever Saknussemm," the professor said, shaking his head. He turned back to Axel. "Hold it up for me, Axel, and I will read it more quickly." The professor leaped onto the table and walked across to where Axel held the parchment next to the lamp.

The professor slowly read aloud: "'Go down into the crater of Sneffels, where the shadow of Scartaris touches, bold traveler, and you will reach the center of the Earth. I did it. Arne Saknussemm.'"

Professor Lidenbrock had no idea how valuable the book was until that moment. In fact, when he had bought the book the day before, he had no clue that it would point the way to such an incredible journey! If what was written on this piece of parchment was true, and he was certain it was, he could follow the great Saknussemm's path. Then there would be no end to the discoveries he could make! It was as if all of his scientific research and studies over the years had prepared him for and led him to that very moment, this very journey! He had no idea of what wonderful mysteries and treasures lay before him, beneath the Earth's surface. One thing *was* certain—he was going to find out! Nothing could stop him!

Professor Lidenbrock leaped off of the table and onto the floor. "Wonderful! Wonderful!" He took three quick steps and leaped into the air. He spun completely around and landed, solidly, on all four paws. "We must start our journey at once!" he announced.

Axel seemed a bit nervous at the thought. The color was draining from his face. It seemed that he wasn't sharing his uncle's excitement. He swallowed hard as he stood and approached the professor. "But, my dear sir, don't you think this note may well be a fake?" he asked timidly.

The professor tried to ignore Axel's doubt and unnecessary fear. He simply replied, "The book in which we have found it is all the proof we need that it is genuine!"

Axel didn't give up that easily. "But, Uncle, what is all this about Sneffels and Scartaris? I have never heard those names before," Axel said with caution.

Professor Lidenbrock couldn't understand why Axel seemed to be so frightened. Why would anyone be afraid to go on such a wonderful expedition? Certainly a journey deep beneath the surface of the Earth would have its dangers. But the chances for discoveries must certainly outweigh any hazards by far, whether real or imaginary. Surely as a scientist, his nephew should realize this. But even if Axel didn't understand the many possibilities right away, Professor Lidenbrock knew the journey itself would surely encourage Axel's sense of discovery and adventure along the way.

It was clear, however, that his nephew needed to be inspired as well as convinced that the note was real. The professor trotted over to a large globe, sitting in a corner of his study, in a wooden floor stand. He turned it slowly with one paw. As he did so, Axel walked over nervously and looked down upon the spinning Earth.

Professor Lidenbrock stopped the spinning globe right at the spot where Iceland faced the two scientists. He then placed his paw beneath a mountain labeled "Sneffels."

"You see, dear boy, Sneffels was once an active volcano. Now, all that remains is an empty crater at its peak. This inactive volcano is about five thousand feet high." He then moved his paw to rest under another mountain, located next to Sneffels, labeled "Scartaris." "And here is the mountain called Scartaris, which is much higher than Sneffels," the professor explained. "It is close enough that its shadow must fall onto a crack or crater inside the mouth of Sneffels. And it is that crater into which we must descend!"

Professor Lidenbrock looked up proudly at Axel.

"We must be off to Iceland, dear nephew," the scientist said as he spun the globe with a flick of his paw. "And from there, we will head to the center of the Earth!"

Axel swallowed hard. From the nervous look upon his face, it was clear that the professor hadn't completely eased his fears.

Chapter Three

The cold ground felt good beneath Professor Lidenbrock's paws as each nail anchored itself firmly into the rock-covered soil. He looked over his shoulder and down the side of Mount Sneffels. The black, volcanic mountain was spread out below him like a huge blanket, stretching to the plains below.

Through the cloudy wisps made by his breath in the icy air, the geologist saw his nephew, Axel, climbing up after him. The professor knew Axel was a skilled climber, but he felt a bit more at ease after checking on him. The professor wagged his tail, and Axel smiled nervously back at him. Professor Lidenbrock turned back to his own climbing. After carefully making another successful step forward, he looked ahead to the large man climbing in front of them—Hans Bjelke, their guide.

The professor and Axel had hired Hans in the town of Reykjavik, Iceland—the last stop on the easy part of their journey. After that fateful day of the discovery of Saknussemm's coded note, Professor Lidenbrock and Axel had traveled for almost an entire month. First, they had gone by train from Hamburg to Denmark. Then, from Denmark, they sailed to Iceland, home of

Mount Sneffels. The inside of that volcano, according to Saknussemm, marked the gateway to the center of the Earth.

In the little port town of Reykjavik, the professor and Axel met Hans, and he agreed to be their guide. Hans spoke Danish, which was one of the many languages Professor Lidenbrock could speak. Looking up at the Icelander, the professor knew that the guide had no idea of the marvelous part he was about to play in the history of the world.

Hans, a calm man of few words, was quite tall, and he had a strong, athletic body. His red hair fit snugly under his hat. Bits of ice were forming in his beard as the chilling wind whipped across his face. Hans was a hunter by trade, but he did not go after the big animals one might expect him to by the look of him.

Hans was a hunter of eider feathers. When the eider ducks of Iceland built their nests, they used the very soft feathers from their chests to line them. Hunters like Hans would collect this down, leaving the unharmed ducks to rebuild their nests. Many people in the far north made their living that way. Eider feathers were known to be among the softest feathers in the world, and wealthy people all over paid high prices for items stuffed with the material.

The professor watched Hans a moment longer. As the eider-feather hunter grasped each rock and took each new step with perfect confidence, Professor Lidenbrock's tail wagged. He was very pleased that he had hired such a skilled guide.

Continuing the climb up the mountain, Hans pulled himself onto a ledge. Then he turned to pull in the loosely hanging rope that linked him to the professor and, in turn, linked the professor to Axel. The professor leaped onto the ledge. Then, grasping the rope in his

mouth, he turned and pulled in the loose portion of rope from between him and Axel. Hans grabbed one of Axel's arms and pulled him easily onto the ledge.

Professor Lidenbrock looked out over the wide plains that surrounded Sneffels. He did not want to stop climbing, but it was clear that his nephew needed to rest. Also, the growling of his stomach told him it was lunchtime. *And I really should not argue with my stomach,* he thought.

Each one took off his heavy knapsack. The three sat quietly, eating their lunch and gazing at the beautiful view from their resting place. The endless Icelandic landscape stretched out before them. They could see deep valleys that crossed one another in every direction. There were smaller mountains that looked like hills. Distant lakes seemed to look more like ponds; ponds looked like puddles, and rivers seemed to change into brooks. To the right, past the plains and valleys, there were glaciers upon glaciers. Many of the peaks were topped with light, fluffy clouds.

The fantastic view meant very little to Professor Lidenbrock. Only one of the peaks, other than the one they were sitting on, interested him. That was Scartaris, the mountain closest to, yet reaching much higher than, Sneffels. More important, it was the only other mountain mentioned in Saknussemm's message. It was the peak whose shadow would point their way.

Professor Lidenbrock was so eager to move on that he wolfed down his food. He was disappointed, however, when Hans insisted they stay put for a good hour in order to rest.

While they waited, the professor wondered why Axel was so quiet. Throughout their journey to Iceland, Axel had tried to talk him out of his quest. "Obsession," his nephew had called it. Axel had told the professor that a journey of five thousand miles to the center of the Earth was impossible. He believed climbing into a volcano, although inactive for over five hundred years, was like crawling into the nose of a cannon, hoping it was not loaded.

Now Axel had fallen silent. The professor had seen him examining certain mineral specimens along the way. Could it be possible Axel had finally been able to see the importance of the truly historical journey they were on? Could Axel finally be realizing that the samples he was finding now would be nothing in comparison to the ones they were bound to discover deep beneath the Earth's surface? Or maybe Axel was quiet because he was just too embarrassed to mention his fears in front of a brave man like Hans. Who knew? Only time would tell. For the moment, Professor Lidenbrock was enjoying the silence.

The rest of the day they spent climbing the inactive volcano. Sometimes they found themselves walking along a well-made path. Most of the time, however, the journey was quite difficult. The dirt and rocks often crumbled right under their feet. Some areas were almost impossible to cross without the travelers helping each other.

When they had reached the beginning of the mountain's ice cap, they thought they would never be able to climb onto the steep, slippery surface. But Hans had an idea. He pointed out some rock outcroppings they could climb on. They made an almost perfect set of natural steps. They had been formed by floods of stones thrown up by Sneffels's many great eruptions. Professor Lidenbrock knew that fate was guiding them to their goal.

The group steadily made their way up the mighty Sneffels. Finally, they reached a large ledge close to the top. The professor called a halt to their trek. "We'll stop here and rest," he said, looking at Axel. They were now over three thousand feet above sea level and had been climbing for many hours. The wind was picking up, and it was clear that Axel was exhausted. It was bitterly cold and the wind was blowing hard. "Maybe we should go ahead and camp here for the night," the professor added, trying to hide his great impatience.

"*Ofvanfor,*" Hans said, shaking his head.

Understanding Hans, the professor turned to Axel. "It seems that we must climb even higher." He turned back to Hans. "Hans, why must we go higher?"

"*Mistour,*" replied the guide, pointing to the plain below.

The professor and Axel looked in the direction where the guide pointed. Below them, they saw a giant column of sand and ground-up stone rising to the heavens. It was a giant tornado slowly swirling its way across the plains below. The storm covered a very large area. Its shadow passed over the three travelers as its monstrous force passed between them and the sun. It was tossing rocks and debris all along its path.

In fact, the violent storm had now left the plains. It began to head up the side of Sneffels, toward the very ledge they were resting on. In just seconds, the tornado was racing over and up the side of the mountain that had taken them long, difficult hours to carefully climb. The professor's fur stood on end. He knew that if this sand spout exploded over them, they would either be crushed in its terrible grip, or swept off the mountain like dust under a mighty broom.

"Hastigt! Hastigt!" cried Hans, as he returned to climbing the sleeping volcano.

This time the professor didn't have to translate. He saw that Axel was already following Hans, even though he was exhausted. The professor hurriedly followed after them. The angry roar of the approaching tornado followed Lidenbrock.

The professor saw where Hans was taking them. Hans was not leading them to the safety of the volcano's crater. Although they had been mountain-climbing for a couple of hours, it would take several more just to reach the top. Hans seemed to be leading them along a path that would take them around the mountain's side.

Professor Lidenbrock realized this was a wise plan. Hans probably knew, as the professor did, that they could never outrun this tornado. But they could cover more ground more quickly if they moved sideways along the volcano, rather than struggling straight up its rocky side. The professor hoped their guide's plan would buy them enough time until the huge storm changed its direction.

As they climbed around the side of Sneffels, the roar of the whirlwind grew louder. The wind gusting around them also increased, making it more difficult to move. Bits of sand and rock had begun to hit them in their

backs. The professor turned to take a curious look back at the approaching storm.

Once more, he was chilled as he witnessed the mighty tornado. It was passing directly over the very spot where he had suggested they stop. Huge stones were pulled from the ground, cast into the air, and thrown around, as if during a volcanic eruption.

Axel gave a small tug on the rope, as he pulled out the slack between him and his uncle. The sudden motion brought the professor back from the hypnotizing motion of the tornado. He quickly turned around and dug in with all fours, desperate to join the others. He was eager to make sure this incredible journey didn't end before it really began.

The wind grew even stronger. The three travelers continued to make their escape. From behind him, the professor heard the deafening roar grow louder and louder. He didn't dare look back. He knew the tornado was right behind him.

Then, with a strange suddenness, the winds faded. Professor Lidenbrock turned to see the *Mistour,* as Hans had called it, travel toward the other side of the volcano.

The storm was moving quickly away from them, churning up everything in its path like a tremendous plow. Its odd movements had worked in their favor. The tornado was now heading back down the mountain and to the plains below. It no longer seemed to be a danger to them. The professor noticed it was already losing some of its force. Soon, he thought, it would calm down to nothing more than a cool breeze.

Professor Lidenbrock returned his gaze to Axel and Hans. He realized that if it wasn't for the great care and knowledge of their guide, they would have all been thrown to the wind just like dust flying from a meteor. Hans decided it would not be safe to camp on the outside of Sneffels. Even though the professor and Axel were tired out from fighting the storm, they agreed with their guide.

It took two more hours for the weary group to reach the top of the volcano. The travelers were so exhausted from the tornado's chase that reaching the top of Sneffels hardly felt like a triumph. Hans picked out an area for their camp just over the top of Sneffels, and a few feet inside the volcano's crater. Having gone just inside the mouth of the volcano, they would be fairly safe from any more of Iceland's *Mistours*. Very tired, everyone ate their supper quietly. Then each traveler found his own space inside the crater's lip and went to sleep.

The professor pawed at his blanket, circled twice, then curled onto his hard, cold bed. Sleeping in the open air five thousand feet above sea level might have been hard for some people. However, the professor's exhaustion made him drop into a deep sleep. With dreams of great adventure and discoveries ahead, he might as well have been curled up next to the cozy fireplace in his home in Hamburg.

The next day, Professor Lidenbrock, Axel, and Hans awoke under the welcome rays of a bright and glorious sun, although the brisk breeze was still freezing. The professor looked out upon the huge circular crater in which they'd slept. The crater of Mount Sneffels was like a giant upside-down cone. It was about half a mile across at the top, and about five hundred feet across at the bottom. Its depth was about two thousand feet. The slope was less steep than the one on the outside of the volcano. The professor hoped they would be able to reach the bottom of the crater's inside without much difficulty.

They gathered up their equipment and ate a light breakfast. Then, once again, they tied themselves together with a long rope and began their descent, with Hans in the lead. In order to make the climb down a bit easier, Hans led them into the crater in a zigzag pattern instead of going straight down.

The ground inside the volcano was much more solid than it was on the outside. The hardened lava they now walked on didn't crumble away underneath them as some of the outside surface had. New muscles in the professor's legs awoke as he climbed down instead of up. It was, however, a pleasant change from the hard climb they made the day before.

Sometimes Hans would come across a large patch of ice draped solidly over the ancient stones. He tested each step carefully. He always watched for hidden cracks and fissures—deep, open gaps in the ice—that might plunge the travelers deep beneath the surface of the frozen snow.

Their trek through the crater's inside held little danger or surprise. Only one of their coils of rope slipped from Axel's grasp and rushed, by a shortcut, to the bottom of the cone.

By midday, the trio had reached the bottom of the crater. Professor Lidenbrock saw Axel as he stared with amazement toward the sky above. Axel seemed to be worried once again. The professor followed Axel's gaze. The upper opening of the cone acted as a circular frame for the sky. The only thing to break up the view was the peak of Scartaris. It seemed lost in the great wide-open space of the heavens. Professor Lidenbrock looked back to Axel. He was peering into the sky as if he thought he would never see it again.

The professor wondered if Axel believed their long climb onto the sleeping volcano would have discouraged the professor from reaching his goal. Of course, the climb up Mount Sneffels was an adventure in itself, but it was only an introduction to the great adventure that lay before them. He wished he could convince his nephew of that fact.

The professor left Axel to watch the sky. He turned to view the inside of the crater. The bottom of the crater was made up of three separate shafts—like chimneys—from which lava had erupted many centuries ago. Wagging his tail, Professor Lidenbrock quickly ran over to examine the shafts, each of which was about one hundred feet in diameter. Axel seemed to keep his distance from the gaping shafts. Hans seated himself on a smooth pile of hardened lava and silently watched the professor tour the open chimneys.

Suddenly, Professor Lidenbrock's tail wagged wildly when he saw what had been carved on an enormous boulder. "Axel! Axel! Come here!" he cried. "Hurry! Wonderful! Wonderful!"

Axel quickly ran over to join his uncle. Once Alex was by his side, Professor Lidenbrock raised a paw to point at the exciting inscription on the stone. The ancient, fading words read: ARNE SAKNUSSEMM.

"Now, Axel," the professor asked, "do you begin to have faith?"

Professor Lidenbrock watched as Axel stepped back, amazed at the discovery. "The evidence cannot be denied—it is truly overwhelming." Axel continued to go back to where he had been. Finally, he reached a clump of hardened lava. Axel followed Hans's example and sat upon it.

The professor moved his gaze from the giant stone to the rim of the crater. He then looked at the peak of the nearby mountain, Scartaris. He caught a quick glimpse of the sun. Then his gaze moved back to the rim of the crater, where Scartaris's shadow had begun to creep.

"Now, we must be patient. As the great Saknussemm has predicted, the shadow of Scartaris will point our way like the needle of a huge compass!" As the professor spoke, his tail wagged more slowly. "There are three paths before us, my friends," he continued. "But only one leads to the inside of the Earth!" The professor trotted over and sat with his two companions.

All three travelers watched as the shadow slowly moved down into Sneffels's crater. The waiting was almost unbearable. Finally, a wave of impatience washed over the professor. He leaped from his seat. Nose to the ground, he followed the shadow every inch of its slow journey. His tail wagged faster and faster as the dark phantom came closer to the three shafts. Finally, as if guided by Saknussemm himself, the shadow of Scartaris fell upon the edge of the central pit.

"Here it is!" gasped the professor, in a moment of absolute joy. "Here it is! We have found it! Forward! Forward!"

Hans rose from his seat. *"Forut,"* the guide said calmly. He began to move their supplies near the dark entrance of the shaft.

With hesitation, Axel got up and approached his uncle and their guide. Then all three stood, gazing into the dark hole. The professor broke the silence. "On this day, June 28, 1863, let the real journey begin! But first, let's take care of our equipment." He turned to the pile of packs that Hans had brought over to them. "They must be divided into four separate bundles."

First, Hans began to separate the supplies into three groups. Then he made a fourth bundle, consisting of their clothes and climbing ropes.

"Hans will take charge of the pickaxes, crowbars, rifle, and gunpowder," the professor said. He turned to his nephew. "Axel, you must take responsibility for the food. I will take care of loading the more delicate instruments like the compass, thermometer, and the manometer, the instrument that measures the pressure of gases or vapors."

Axel helped Hans divide their bags. Meanwhile, the professor carefully gathered the scientific instruments with his mouth and placed them into his own knapsack.

Axel then looked over to the fourth pile. "But, Uncle," he said, "what about our clothes and all of this rope? Who will carry them down into the shaft?"

The professor pulled the last strap on his pack tight with his teeth. He then looked up at Axel. "They will go down by themselves," he said. He looked over to Hans, who had already finished putting together his pack. He had begun to bundle the fourth pile tightly.

"How?" asked Axel.

"You shall see," Professor Lidenbrock replied, as Hans looked to the professor, who simply nodded his head. Hans then tossed the package over the edge of the hole.

Both Professor Lidenbrock and Axel knelt side by side and leaned over the edge of the pit. The professor heard the rush of air and the noise of fallen stones as the descending bundle bounced off one of the walls. Then it completely disappeared deep into the darkness. They watched and listened a bit longer, but only silence remained.

Professor Lidenbrock turned to look at Axel. His nephew's face was now only inches away from his own. "Now, then," he whispered, "it's our turn."

Wow! I bet that pit goes a long way down! We didn't even hear the bundle of clothes and ropes hit the bottom! That just goes to prove that sometimes you have to dig really deep to reach your goal.

Speaking of digging deep, it's time to check on our little piece of buried treasure back in Oakdale!

Chapter Four

Joe's mom, Ellen Talbot, held the mysterious metal disk under the stream of warm water coming from the kitchen faucet. Small pieces of dirt and mud began to fall away. The earthy odor made its way over to Wishbone.

The dog was getting a very nice scratch behind the ears from Sam. She and Joe were sitting at the kitchen table enjoying a couple of glasses of lemonade. Sam had always been the best at ear-scratching. But the smell coming from the kitchen sink pulled the dog away from Sam. He went over to the kitchen counter, next to Ellen. Wishbone raised himself up and placed his two front paws on the edge of the counter. He tried to get a better look at the action, as well as a better smell.

"Well, Mrs. Talbot?" David asked. He was standing on the other side of Joe's mom.

"I can't seem to get all the dirt off," Ellen replied. She continued to rub her fingers over the remaining dirt clumps that were still left on the artifact, which was now more easy to see.

Wishbone blew out a quick breath. "And why would you want to get all the dirt off?" he asked.

Ellen turned the hot-water knob, increasing the

water's temperature. The slender, brown-haired woman scraped at a stubborn piece of dirt with her fingernail.

"Hey!" Wishbone's tail wagged. "I found the thing. I say we leave the dirt on . . . for added flavor."

Paying no attention, Ellen held up the small piece of round metal into the sunlight coming through the kitchen window. The small, wet disk glistened in her hand. "Take a look at this," she said, as David moved closer. "One side is plain. The other side has an inscription in the center of it."

"Can you see what it says?" David asked, leaning even closer. Wishbone also stretched up onto the toes of his hind paws, trying to get a closer look.

"Well, I don't know for sure." Ellen tilted the disk in her hand so the sunlight would hit the finely written inscription. Then she said, "But I can certainly tell you that it's written in Latin."

"You studied Latin in school, didn't you, Mom?" Joe asked, as he and Sam came over to the sink. Everyone's eyes were glued to the artifact in Ellen's hand.

"I studied Latin half-a-zillion years ago, in high school," Ellen replied, laughing a bit.

Wishbone's ears perked up. "You're *that* old?" His eyes went from Ellen's hand to her face. *I wonder how long that is in dog years.*

Ellen squinted her eyes as she tried to make out the inscription. "Let's see . . . *honoris* . . . 'of honor.'"

"That's what I was thinking," Wishbone added.

"Then . . ." Ellen kept reading. "*Fortitudine* . . . Oh— fortitude . . . strength!"

"That would have been my guess," Wishbone said, as he grew a bit impatient. *Being able to speak another language is all well and good, but I find digging much more fun. And there's plenty more of that waiting outside.*

"I can't tell you much about the rest," Ellen admitted. She lowered the disk back into the stream of running water.

David leaned over and pointed to another inscription. "What's that?" he asked. "There—at the bottom."

Ellen lifted the disk out of the water again. "Well, it looks like initials." She read the inscription. "It says 'N. J.'"

"Maybe it's a piece of jewelry," Sam said, looking over Ellen's shoulder.

"And maybe this 'N. J.' person owned it," David added, as Ellen handed him the metal to examine.

This time he held it in the sunlight. As he turned it, the sun's rays hit the inscription, making it sparkle and seem to leap off of the dull disk.

"Maybe we've found something really rare and valuable." David's eyes lit up as he spoke. "Archaeologists dig up cool stuff all the time. They find ancient pottery, tools, even animal fossils—right under the ground we walk on every day!"

"I know, but this is Oakdale. It's not Egypt or some really old place like that," Joe added.

"Hey, everyone," Sam said, "face it, we won't know for sure until we find out what this is. What do we do next?"

Wishbone barked. "Exactly what we've *been* doing, people! Let's go back outside and keep digging up the original site!" He wagged his tail wildly. "Read my lips! Dig! Dig!"

Ellen knelt down and opened the double doors under the sink. She began to rummage through the cabinet.

Wishbone dropped his front paws to the floor. "No, Ellen!" Wishbone barked again. "Dig in the *hole*—not in the cabinet!" He sighed and turned a circle. No one ever listened to the dog.

Seeing that Wishbone was alarmed, Sam knelt and rubbed him behind one ear. "What's wrong, boy? Maybe you're just excited. You might have finally found something valuable this time."

Sam's scratching made Wishbone forget about his communication problem. Instead, he stuck out his chest proudly. "That's me and my nose," he said, "boldly going where no dog has gone before!"

Ellen pulled a small, funny-smelling metal container out of the cabinet. She set it on the countertop. She then opened a cabinet above the counter and took out a small white bowl.

Wishbone watched as she opened the funny-smelling can and poured its even worse-smelling blue liquid into the bowl.

"What's that?" Sam asked.

"Well, since this disk might be a piece of jewelry, I thought I'd try some jewelry-cleaning solution," Ellen replied. David handed her the metal disk, and she dipped it into the solution.

"Uh . . . don't expect me to put that thing back in my mouth," Wishbone said, placing his front paws on the cabinet at the sink.

Ellen took a small cloth and began to rub it over the surface of the mysterious disk. She made sure to keep the piece in the solution the whole time. Everyone watched as most of the remaining dirt fell away from the now brighter piece of metal. The many tiny particles of dirt that had clogged its tiny crevices dissolved or fell to the bottom of the bowl. The inscription became easier to see.

David peered into the bowl. "I think this solution is working!" he said excitedly.

Wishbone watched as Ellen continued to rub the disk with the cloth. She then raised it out of the bowl and held what looked like an entirely different object into the light of the sun. The inscription glistened more brightly off of the wet, golden background. Wishbone turned to see a small golden circle dance across the opposite kitchen wall as the tiny disk reflected the afternoon sun.

Ellen examined the disk a bit closer. Using one of her fingernails, this time, instead of scraping off dirt, she pressed it hard into an edge of the piece. She pulled it away to reveal a small dent left by the pressure of her fingernail. "It's soft," she said, examining the dent. "I think this piece is gold."

"Gold?" David asked excitedly.

Wishbone gave a small bark. "Hot diggety dog!"

"Hey! Maybe it's part of some pirate's buried treasure!" Joe said, turning to Sam.

"Right!" she agreed. "But we're not near an ocean."

Ellen turned the disk over in her hand. "Well, it's definitely quite a mystery."

"I found gold!" Wishbone said. "I'm rich!" Wishbone circled on the kitchen floor. His mind raced, just thinking of all the things he could buy with his new fortune. "Let's see, I could get some more tennis balls, even some more chew toys—mine are kind of soggy." He looked up at Joe and Ellen. "Don't worry, this rich dog won't forget about you two. I'm going to buy each of you your very own, special, one-of-a-kind . . . tug-of-war ropes! That way, you can play tug-of-war with your favorite dog—me!" His tail wagged wildly. "Isn't that great?"

"I bet that inscription holds the key to whatever it is," Joe pointed out.

"Maybe it's from some secret society," Sam said with a gleam in her eye.

The kids were getting more and more excited about the discovery. Once again, David took the golden disk and examined it closely. "You're right. The inscription could be some kind of code!" Smiling, he looked at Joe and Sam, then turned to face Ellen. "Can you translate some more, Mrs. Talbot?"

Ellen shook her head. "No, I'm sorry. I wish I remembered more of my Latin."

"What are we going to do?" Sam asked. Her sense of excitement seemed to be going away.

"Mom," Joe said, "do you still have your old Latin textbook?"

"No," Ellen answered. Then suddenly an idea came to her. Her face lit up. "I just might still have an old Latin dictionary."

The kids' hopes clearly lifted again. Then, it was David's turn to express an idea. "Hey," he said, "let's go to the library and check out some Oakdale history books!"

Sam finished his thought. "You're right. We can find out what has happened around this area in the past!"

"Who knows," Joe said, "maybe there *were* pirates around Oakdale at some time!"

David handed the disk back to Ellen. Ellen placed it onto a clean dishcloth to dry. "While you do that," she said, "I'll spend some time in the basement and dig around for that dictionary."

"Did someone say *dig?*" Wishbone looked up at Ellen, his tongue hanging out. "I will stay here and help you, Ellen!" The dog loved to nose around in the basement—all those interesting old smells and old memories. To Wishbone, a trip down to the basement was an adventure in itself.

"Okay, Mom," Joe said, finishing his lemonade. "We'll see you in about an hour."

Joe and Sam placed their empty glasses in the kitchen sink. Then they left with David out the back door. Wishbone heard the clatter of them picking up their bikes. Then came the more rhythmic ticking and pedaling as the trio rode off down the street toward downtown. He looked up at Ellen, who was drying her hands.

"Okay, Wishbone," she said, walking toward the back of the kitchen. "Let's see what we can find." Ellen opened the narrow door that was directly underneath the staircase leading upstairs.

Wishbone trotted over and looked through the open doorway. Below him, a flight of steps led downward, into darkness. Above him, Ellen flicked the switch that would light up the basement, but nothing happened. She flipped it on and off a few times.

"Looks like the bulb is out," Ellen said to herself. She walked over to the kitchen counter, opened a drawer, and pulled out a flashlight. Then she returned to the open doorway. "I guess we have to do this mostly in the dark, Wishbone," Ellen said. She turned on the flashlight and descended into the basement. A bright shaft of light danced ahead of her. The light from the flashlight reflected off the tiny dust particles floating through the basement air.

Wishbone didn't mind the dark. He followed Ellen down the staircase eagerly. He thought going into a dark basement was kind of exciting. It was definitely better than counting ceiling tiles all day.

Cool! A mysterious gold disk! I wonder who it belonged to, or what it was made for. Maybe the answers are in the basement, at the bottom of these dark stairs.

Hey! You know what? Descending into the unknown darkness was just what Professor Lidenbrock had to do!

Chapter Five

Professor Lidenbrock watched as Axel slowly lowered himself down into the darkness below. The dim light glowing from the Ruhmkorf coil lantern hanging from Axel's belt lit up a small circle of rock near where he descended.

The professor thought they were very lucky to have the Ruhmkorf coils. They were a special lamp invented by the chemist M. Ruhmkorf. They did not use oil or gas, but electricity. Each came with its own battery. The coil could easily be worn on a climber's sturdy belt. Carrying the coils was much easier than traveling around with a big, heavy supply of lamp oil.

Although the professor couldn't see Hans, he calculated that the guide stood waiting on a ledge about two hundred feet below the one where he was. Both the professor and Hans had turned their lamps off. That way, they could save battery power and also avoid blinding Axel during his descent.

Professor Lidenbrock was very happy to be away from Iceland's cold wind. The temperature of the volcano's interior was more regular, and also comfortable. No sudden blasts of wind would hit them there. Even the ice that had built up on his fur had melted away soon after they had begun their trek into the shaft's darkness.

Together, the three travelers had been descending into Saknussemm's dark pit at about two hundred feet at a time. In between each descent, they rested. The longest rope they had was four hundred feet. In order to reuse the rope, they had looped the center of it around a sturdy rock outcropping. That left two equal lengths of rope, each slightly less than two hundred feet long, to dangle in the darkness.

Hans and Axel had then descended by holding onto both lengths of rope. The professor used a somewhat different method. When Axel and Hans had reached each new ledge below, they would then lower down the professor.

"Uncle," came Axel's voice from below, "I'm on the ledge." His shouts bounced off the sides of the tunnel's shaft and up to the professor's keen ears.

"Very well," Professor Lidenbrock answered. "Slowly pull on one end of the rope." The professor turned on his lamp. It lit his section of the deep hole. He looked down and watched as the rope slid around a large rock sticking out from the ledge he was standing on.

When the end of the rope came into view, the professor called to Axel to stop pulling. He cautiously took the short end of the rope into his mouth and grasped it hard between his teeth. Pulling the rope tightly against the rock, the professor turned his body around, with his back facing the hole, and slowly began to step backward—off the ledge. His front paws dug into the top of the ledge as his hind legs began to feel their way backward down the rock wall.

"All vright, Axshel!" the professor yelled. The rope in his mouth made him slur his words. "Lowver me tdown!"

Below, he could hear Hans and Axel's hands slide

along the tightened rope as he continued to walk backward down the rocky slope. Above him, he could hear the rope slide against the rock. Bits of dirt and stone fell onto his head from above. But his grip was as strong as a bear trap, and he held on tightly as his guide and nephew slowly lowered him down to the next ledge.

For nine more hours, they repeated the same movements. Each time, the opening they had entered slowly shrank away until it was just a small dot above them.

Slowly, they approached the bottom of the giant pit. At the beginning of their decent, only the professor's keen hearing could pick up any sort of noise. Now, they all could clearly hear the stones and lava that they knocked loose hit the hard floor of the pit below. As the last stone fell, it was clear to Professor Lidenbrock that they were on the final ledge.

The professor backed down the steep wall one last

time. His nails scraped at the hard surface. As he moved, he calculated the distance they had descended into Mount Sneffels. They had shifted their rope twenty-eight times, and their doubled rope had been almost two hundred feet long. Twenty-eight times two hundred feet equaled a total of five thousand six hundred feet. They had descended more than a mile into the shaft!

— When Professor Lidenbrock was just a few feet above the bottom of the pit, he pushed away from the wall with all fours. As the rope swung away from the side, the professor loosened his jaws. He released his tight grip on the rope and let himself drop neatly to the ground. He looked up at his nephew. "We have reached the end of our journey," he said.

— Hans didn't seem to pay attention. He just gathered the rope. However, Axel's face lit up with excitement and wonder. "We have? You mean we've reached the interior of the Earth?" he asked.

Professor Lidenbrock sighed. It was clear their amazing descent had not raised Axel's spirits. "No, Axel," the professor replied. "We have reached the bottom of this giant well."

"And I suppose we can go no farther?" he asked hopefully.

Professor Lidenbrock turned a slow circle. His lamp threw a small circle of light cross the bottom of the pit. As the professor turned, the light lit up nothing but the hardened lava wall. But, finally, the light came to rest over the entrance to a dark tunnel. Its opening was visible for just a few feet before it turned sharply to the right.

"Look there, Axel!" the professor exclaimed. "There before you is a tunnel—and the next leg of our journey." He turned from facing the tunnel to look at Axel. Hans was now packing the rope into his knapsack. "In any event, we must see about that tomorrow. We have spent the entire day climbing down, two hundred feet at a time. Let us now eat and have a good night's rest."

The three travelers ate a light supper. Then each did his best to make a bed among the piles of stones, dirt, and lava that had gathered through the years at the bottom of the volcano's shaft. The professor watched as Hans cleared away an area, then laid his blanket over the hard surface. Axel stretched himself over some ropes and clothes they had thrown down earlier. Each seemed eager for sleep after a long day's work.

Professor Lidenbrock made some notations in a leather-bound book he carried and then curled up snugly on his blanket. He turned his gaze upward toward the top of the long shaft. A single brilliant star shone through the small opening at the top. It was as if he were looking through a giant telescope. The professor made a few calculations in his head. He believed it was a star from the constellation of the Little Bear. After doing his little bit of astronomy, Professor Lidenbrock fell into a sound sleep.

The next morning, the three travelers awoke inside the dark shaft. Hans switched on his lamp and handed out food and water. Everyone ate a light breakfast of biscuits and dried meat.

In between mouthfuls of biscuit, Professor Lidenbrock turned to Axel. "Well, Axel, my boy," he asked, "what say you now? Did you ever spend a more peaceful night in our house in Hamburg?" He looked around the cavern. "No deafening sounds of cart wheels, no yelling from cats at all hours!"

"Well, Uncle," Axel replied, "it is truly very quiet at

the bottom of this well." He took a sip of water from his canteen, then continued. "But, to me, there is something alarming in all this calm."

"Why, one would say you were nervous," the professor said, finishing off the last of his breakfast. "Did you know that, as yet, we have not gone even one inch into the depths of the Earth?"

Axel looked puzzled. "What can you mean, sir?"

"I mean to say," the professor answered, "that we have only just reached the bottom of the island of Iceland. This long vertical tube, which begins at the crater of Sneffels, ends roughly at sea level."

"Are you sure, Uncle?" Axel asked.

"Absolutely," the professor replied, looking at his notes. "Sneffels is about a mile high, and we have plunged just over a mile into its stomach." Professor Lidenbrock stood. "Now that we have had our breakfast, let us quickly be on our way."

The professor placed his blanket in his knapsack. Meanwhile, Hans and Axel packed their own gear. Then they divided equally the remaining supplies and equipment. Everyone had their packs on their backs. Hans and Axel held the pickaxes in their hands. Then the three travelers switched on their lamps and walked toward the tunnel entrance.

"Now, Axel," the professor said enthusiastically, "we are about to take our first step into the interior of the Earth!"

Hans led the way. The professor went next, followed by Axel. The passage wound around and down into the Earth. Professor Lidenbrock stepped closer to the tunnel's wall to get a better look at what it was made of. The light from his lamp bounced off the deep black walls and pierced into its many small dark holes. Some parts of the wall looked like Swiss cheese. The professor believed that, long ago, a stream of fiery lava flowing from the Earth's core had carved a passageway through the tunnel. The hardened lava now lined the inside of the tunnel with its thick coating.

The tunnel itself was just a bit wider than the hallways in the professor's house back in Hamburg. Looking through the tunnel was not at all like looking down the stairway at his house. The tunnel was generally not that steep. Nevertheless, it did appear to be leading gradually downward.

At some points, however, the passageway *was* very steep. Once again, the group had to tie a length of rope between them and help one another make their way down the slope. Most of the passageway, however, was little more than a leisurely stroll. Large holes in the hardened lava ground often served as steps. It was as if they were leading the travelers slowly down into a dark basement.

As the three made their way, the tunnel widened and the scenery became much more interesting.

Long ago, the professor guessed, the tunnel had been filled with moisture. Water dripping from the ceiling carried with it small amounts of calcium. The calcium deposits would, over many years, build up into large stalactites. They looked like giant icicles made of rock. Directly below some of them, upside-down rock icicles called stalagmites grew upward from the ground to meet the stalactites. They were formed as extra calcium in the water dripped off the tips of the stalactite directly overhead.

All around the trio, the light from their lamps refracted and reflected off the many crystals jutting out of the solidified lava. That lava existed in a whole range of colors—from reddish brown to pale yellow. When the light would strike the tunnel's walls, the crystals themselves would glow.

It thrilled Professor Lidenbrock to watch Axel as he examined each mineral display with a complete sense of joy. He used his pickaxe to chip away small samples. Then he placed them in the specimen bag he kept slung about his neck. It seemed that Axel had forgotten his fears at least for a moment. Perhaps he was beginning to understand the wonderful possibilities of this trip.

Professor Lidenbrock believed Axel's sense of discovery should be encouraged. "Wait until we advance farther, Axel." As the professor spoke, his voice echoed off the solidified lava. "What we have discovered up till now is nothing. Onward, my boy! Onward!"

With Hans in the lead, the three travelers descended deeper into the lava-carved tunnel. They trekked all of that day. Even though the tunnel always led farther downward, they never seemed to make their way out of the lava tube. They were still surrounded by the hard rock. The professor had believed soft dirt would surely wait for them below the ancient volcano.

At about eight o'clock in the evening, Professor Lidenbrock gave the signal to halt. They had made great progress—reaching a depth of ten thousand feet below sea level. They stopped inside a large cavern the size of a great ballroom. Each hung his lamp onto an outcropping of rock in the lava wall. The long, unending march into the Earth had once again made the travelers tired and hungry.

It was clear from Axel's look of relief that he was glad his uncle had declared the day's journey over. Hans began to unpack their supplies. Then he laid out onto a block of lava what was to be their dinner.

Each ate in silence. As Professor Lidenbrock chewed his food with pleasure, he watched Axel. He, too, enjoyed the rest and his food. But after Axel had taken a sip from his canteen, that same troubled look the professor had grown so used to seeing returned to his nephew's face.

"What's the matter, dear boy?" he asked between mouthfuls. "Does your dinner not suit you?"

Axel looked to Hans, who was sitting and eating in his usual manner, relaxed and quiet. Then Axel turned his gaze to his uncle. "I am quite uneasy that we certainly do not have enough water to last for more than a few days," he said, placing the cork back into his canteen.

"Is that all?" the professor asked. Then he said, "Don't worry on the matter. I still believe we shall find plenty of water—in fact, far more than we shall want."

"But when?" Axel asked.

"When we finally get past this layer of lava crust," the professor replied. "How can you expect springs to force their way through these solid stone walls?"

Axel just stared at his uncle. The three quietly finished their dinner and went to sleep.

For five more days the group traveled through the tunnel of lava. On the third day, Professor Lidenbrock placed Hans in charge of dividing up their food. They had enough supplies to last for several months, with one big exception. The professor had counted on finding underground streams soon after their journey began, so the travelers had not packed much water. On the fifth day, they had used up the last few mouthfuls of their supply.

However, Professor Lidenbrock was not going to give up on his quest. No matter that his dry throat burned or his weak muscles ached, he was determined to continue onward. He tried to ignore the fact that his dehydrated body told him to stop. Even his nose had been dry for the past two days. Nothing, however, was going to keep him from following Saknussemm's path.

Several times, Axel tried to make his uncle reconsider his quest. However, any argument on Axel's part was ignored. Any reason he gave for turning back fell on his uncle's deaf, furred ears. The professor was disappointed to see that Axel's courage ran dry, along with the water supply.

For the next two days, the weary travelers continued down the dark, stony corridor. Still, all that surrounded them was the hard, solidified lava. Their pace had slowed considerably. They had to stop and rest more often.

Finally, on the eighth day of their underground trek, Axel could take no more. The passage had taken them upward, downward, and then in a horizontal direction. Then downward again . . . Although Hans seemed hardly affected by the lack of water, and the professor's progress was merely slowed, Axel had dropped to his knees and had fallen forward. Panting a little, his tongue hanging from his open mouth, Professor Lidenbrock walked to where his nephew lay and gently rolled him over. Axel opened his eyes and sat up.

"Poor boy," the professor said. "Reach into my pack."

Axel did as his uncle said. He pulled a small flask from the pack.

"Drink, dear nephew," the professor said quietly. "It's the very last mouthful. I saved it for you—in an emergency." He watched as Axel put the mouth of the flask next to his cracked lips and slowly drank the last few drops. "Yes, my dear boy," the professor continued, "I knew that if you would fall down half dead, this last drop of water would revive you."

"Thank you, dear Uncle," Axel replied. "Thank you from my heart."

After the last few drops trickled into Axel's mouth, he placed the small flask back into the professor's pack and stood.

"Well!" Axel said with joy. "There can be no doubt now as to what we have to do."

The professor's heart soared. He knew that the water would give his nephew new life!

Axel continued. "Water has completely failed us. Our journey is therefore at an end. Let us end the journey at once."

The professor's heart dropped like a stone. "Go back?" he questioned surprisingly.

"Yes," Axel responded, "and we must not lose a single moment. May heaven give us strength for us, once more, to revisit the light of day."

Professor Lidenbrock could not believe what he was hearing. "So, my dear Axel," he said, "those few drops of water have not restored your energy and courage?"

"Courage!" Axel exclaimed. "You are not discouraged, sir?"

The professor was totally surprised by the question. "What?" he cried. "And give up just as we are on the verge of success?" He placed his two front paws onto Axel's legs. "Never, never shall it be said that Professor Lidenbrock retreated!"

Axel, his back to the smooth stone wall, slowly slid down until he was sitting. A look of complete hopelessness washed over his face. "Then we must make up our minds to die," he said with a sigh.

Professor Lidenbrock placed a paw onto Axel's hand. "No, Axel, certainly not," he said quietly. "Go back. Leave me. I don't want you to be hurt." The professor pawed Axel's hand very slowly in an attempt to comfort him. It had no effect. "Take Hans with you. I will go on alone."

"You ask us to leave you?" Axel asked, dumbfounded.

Professor Lidenbrock stepped back and turned away from Axel. "Leave me, I say. I was the one who decided to undertake this dangerous adventure. I will continue to the end, or I will never return to the surface of Mother Earth." He faced Axel once again. "Go, Axel! Once more I say to you—go!"

He watched as Axel said nothing. The young man just looked toward the hard ground. Professor Lidenbrock's eyes left Axel in search of their guide. However, he was nowhere to be seen. The professor looked down the tunnel behind them, then up ahead of them. Not even the glow from Hans's lamp could be seen. He turned back to Axel.

"Where is Hans?" the professor asked.

Then, as if his question had been answered, he heard the distant sound of footsteps—boots running on solid rock. He turned to face the tunnel ahead of him after he made out a distant dim light. Now the footsteps were close enough for Axel to hear. He, too, turned to face the lighted pathway. He slowly stood.

The glow of the light and sound of the footsteps grew. Finally, Hans came into full view. As soon as he saw the other two travelers watching, he yelled, "*Vatten!*"

"What?" Axel asked, sounding as if he were in a daze.

"*Vatten! Vatten!*" Hans repeated with the most excitement he had shown during the entire journey.

Axel turned to the professor. "What is he saying?"

Professor Lidenbrock looked proudly at Axel. "He said *water!*"

Hans motioned for the other two to follow. Axel and the professor quickly ran after him with renewed strength.

Together they ran down the long tunnel for about a hundred yards. Then Professor Lidenbrock began to hear a dull sound, like that of a distant waterfall. "Hans is right!" he said enthusiastically. "That is the low rumble of either a torrent or a flood!"

Axel's face lit up with joy. Everyone's pace quickened.

"There's not the slightest doubt about it," the professor continued. "An underground river is flowing right near us!"

As they progressed, the roar became louder and louder, finally almost deafening. Then, as they kept running, the roar began to fade. It was clear they were passing their only chance for survival.

Hans suddenly stopped. Then he began to move back the way they had come. When he had reached the spot where the roar seemed to be the loudest, he placed an ear to the wall. It was obvious to the professor that the guide was looking for the exact spot where the noise of the torrent was loudest. When he had found what he was looking for, the Icelander took the pickaxe from his belt and began to strike the wall with controlled patience.

It wasn't long before a welcome bubbling was heard. Through the hole Hans had made, a jet of water burst with such force that it struck the opposite wall of the tunnel.

Axel plunged his hand directly into the stream, only to pull it back in pain. "Boiling!" he cried, turning to the professor.

Professor Lidenbrock trotted over to a small puddle that had already formed on the tunnel's floor. "Well, never mind," he said, "it will soon cool off against the cold ground."

The tunnel began to fill with clouds of vapor, while a small stream flowed off into the interior of the Earth. Soon, everyone gathered around the professor and the small puddle. All three travelers bent and lapped away at the cool water. *The only way to drink,* the professor thought.

After they had drunk all they could, everyone filled their canteens. "Perhaps we should try to close this hole so the water does not run out completely," Axel said, as he replaced the cork to his canteen.

"Why must we go through such trouble?" the professor asked. Then he answered his own question. "When our canteens are empty, we are not at all sure that we shall be able to fill them again from where we will be. Plus I don't think the water source will dry up."

"I think you are correct," Axel replied.

"Well, then," the professor continued, "let this water run. It will, of course, run downward, the same path we are following. It will serve to guide and refresh us."

A smile rose from Axel's lips. "I think the idea is a good one," he said. "In fact, since Hans discovered this underground river, let us name it after him. That is the usual custom of explorers."

"A splendid idea, dear nephew," the professor said. He pulled out his book, wrote a few notes, then returned the book to his pack. "Hans River it is!"

Professor Lidenbrock looked over to Hans. Having had his fill of water, he had seated himself on a rock with his usual calm manner. Somehow, he seemed not a bit more proud than he was before.

"And with Hans River as our companion," Axel continued, "there is no further reason why we should not succeed in our marvelous adventure."

"Ah, my boy!" Professor Lidenbrock laughed as happiness filled him. "After all, you are coming around." He turned his gaze to Hans, then back to Axel. "Then let us continue on our most incredible journey!"

Chapter Six

Soon after the discovery of Hans River, the three travelers began to emerge from the surrounding lava. Layers of very old soil began to appear, mixed in among the hardened lava. And as they descended, the hardened lava all but disappeared.

No explorers had ever found themselves placed in such a position to study nature in all her true beauty. Throughout the tunnel walls there were streaks of copper, manganese, platinum, and gold. The light from the Ruhmkorf coils seemed to brighten beyond belief as it bounced off all of the brilliantly colored rocks and appeared to send jets of fire in every direction.

This time Axel was in the lead. It seemed his fear had left him as he led the group farther into the depths of the Earth.

For eleven more days they traveled in a leisurely manner. The runoff from Hans River was at their feet, guiding and refreshing them. Professor Lidenbrock hardly touched his canteen anymore. Whenever he would become thirsty, he would simply lower his head and lap up the refreshing water Hans River offered.

Sometimes, on the very steep descents, the river's

waters would turn into a raging waterfall. Its mighty roar equaled the professor's own obsession to reach the Earth's core. But most of the time, the cavern's downward direction was gradual enough that the Hans River ran along as quietly and calmly as the man for whom it was named.

On the twentieth day after they entered the shaft, Professor Lidenbrock stopped to check his notes and calculations. Hans stopped, as well. Once again he found a large rock to sit upon. Axel was in the lead, and still moving on. The professor peered ahead through the tunnel, but he saw only darkness. He wasn't worried, however. No doubt Axel's lamplight was hidden around a corner, and the beam was swallowed up by the tunnel's darkness. No matter. The professor would not take long to finish his notes and calculations. He and Hans would catch up to Axel soon enough.

Professor Lidenbrock slipped his pack off and nudged open the top flap. He reached into it and, with his teeth, gently pulled out a small leather-bound book. He had been entering into the book every angle of descent, and every compass and manometer reading. He laid the book on the hard ground, being careful not to place it too close to where the waters of Hans River flowed. He opened the volume and flipped through the pages with his nose.

As he went over all the notes and measurements listed, he couldn't believe what he suddenly realized. According to his calculations, they had already traveled *ninety miles* below the Earth's surface! They were also no longer under Sneffels or even Iceland.

They had been traveling directly under the Atlantic Ocean for some time! At that very moment, there could be fierce storms raging miles above them on the ocean's surface. Or there could be giant whales cruising near the bottom of the sea—a bottom that was now the roof over their heads.

This is exciting! Professor Lidenbrock closed the book and replaced it into his pack. "We must find Axel," he told Hans. "He will be very surprised to learn that the three of us are walking under the Atlantic Ocean!"

The professor and Hans went farther down the passage in search of Axel. The last time they had seen him, he was examining and collecting samples of different layers of ancient granite. Professor Lidenbrock trotted along, eager to tell Axel the good news.

The two companions continued down the ancient tunnel for almost an hour. Still there was no sign of Axel. The professor was sure they should have caught up to him by then.

"Axel!" the professor called loudly. "Axel! Where are you, my dear boy?"

Only the quiet babbling of the stream from Hans River answered.

For another half hour they searched. Professor Lidenbrock became more concerned. "Hans," he said urgently, "try firing a shot with your rifle. Perhaps that sound will carry farther than our voices." The professor sat down and watched as Hans went into action.

Hans removed the rifle and powder horn that were slung over his shoulder. He carefully poured a sufficient amount of powder down the barrel. With a rod, he plunged a wad of cloth into the barrel. The professor noticed that Hans didn't add a lead ball. He thought that was a wise idea. After all, it was possible that the bullet would ricochet around the tiny cavern and make its way to Axel, or even back to them.

Hans aimed the rifle toward the top of the tunnel and fired. The roar was deafening as the sound vibrated and echoed off the walkway. The sound was especially loud to the professor, with his keen hearing. When Hans prepared to fire another shot, Professor Lidenbrock quickly placed his paws over his ears.

After Hans had fired the rifle once more, they both listened carefully for a response. The echoing sound of the rifle was getting fainter as it bounced around the corridor. When the noise had finally stopped, all the professor could hear was the soft sound of Hans River running beside their feet—that and the slight ringing in his ears from Hans's first shot. He wished he had covered his ears for that first shot. The professor promised not to let himself again be so wrapped up in his work that he would forget to pay attention to common sense.

Professor Lidenbrock hoped Axel was all right. There were, no doubt, many dangers he could have run into. The professor had confidence in his nephew's abilities. However, any one of the travelers would be in more danger by himself than with the other two.

The professor was very concerned for Axel's safety. No journey, no matter how incredible, would be worth the loss of his nephew's life. The professor knew he couldn't live with himself if his quest for discovery brought harm to his dear nephew, Axel.

Professor Lidenbrock sat listening for some response from Axel. He then realized that he had ignored another matter of common sense. And it was not just a question of common sense, but his sense of smell. That was it! The professor had an unusually strong sense of smell! As he placed his nose to the ground, he realized that he should have thought of that before.

He took in a deep breath of the dusty ground through his sensitive nostrils. He smelled scents from himself and from Hans, but not from Axel. He sniffed around some more and realized the awful truth—Axel had not traveled down this passageway. There wasn't a trace of his nephew's scent anywhere.

Could it be true? The professor knew that Axel had been in front of them. Could he and Hans, during their search, have passed a tunnel leading off of the main passageway? Could they have mistaken this passageway for one of the many shadows that they passed? That had to be the answer!

"Axel did not travel this far, Hans," the professor said confidently. "We must retrace our steps!" With his nose to the ground, Professor Lidenbrock trotted back up the gentle slope of the passageway. "Keep firing your rifle, Hans! I want Axel to know that help is on the way!"

Together, the pair continued their backward journey in the sloping tunnel for almost an hour. Professor Lidenbrock ran faster and faster, putting more distance between himself and Hans. Once again, he let his emotions get the best of him. When he realized this, he stopped and quickly pointed his nose at the ground. He smelled traces of himself, Hans, and . . . Axel! He took a few more sniffs to be sure. It was Axel, all right. The professor had found his nephew's trail!

Behind him, he heard Hans's rifle fire again. He didn't have to place his paws over his ears this time. His running had put some distance between him and the eider-feather hunter.

Professor Lidenbrock began to make his way back down the tunnel toward Hans. His nose to the ground, he was trying to find the spot where Axel had become separated from him and their guide. As he went, his eyes looked ahead of him to see the glow of Hans's lamp rounding a corner. Soon after, the professor could make out the figure of the trusty guide as he approached. He was pouring powder down the barrel of his rifle for another shot.

"Hold your fire, Hans," Professor Lidenbrock said, trotting over to him quickly. "I feel we are very close to where Axel lost his way!"

Once the professor had reached Hans, he placed his nose to the ground. Once again, however, he smelled only his and Hans's trail. He turned and looked back down the tunnel. All he saw behind him was a single, narrow passageway.

"Hans," the professor said, as he slowly stepped through the empty passageway, "hold your lamp out high and move it around slowly." Hans did as he was told, and he cautiously followed the professor. Professor Lidenbrock watched the shadows move and sway with the movement of the light. The tunnel had many rock outcroppings that cast deep shadows from both of their lamps. However, as they approached, most of the swaying shadows disappeared. The professor was looking for one particular shadow that would not disappear when they approached.

And he found it! It was ahead of them, on the right, just behind a large outgrowth of rock that went from top to bottom. A tall shadow didn't sway in the moving lamplight, and it remained dark when they approached. Professor Lidenbrock turned to face the shadow. His lamplight opened up the darkness. It was another passageway!

There was one thing that puzzled the professor. He walked past the new tunnel's entrance. Then he turned to look at it from another direction.

"Fascinating," the professor said to himself. When he looked back down the tunnel, all he saw was the guide, Hans. He stood in the middle of what looked like a wall. There was an outcropping of rock on both sides of the tunnel entrance. It made the new cavern almost invisible, unless someone was standing right beside it.

"Quite an optical illusion," Professor Lidenbrock said shaking his head.

Hans walked over to where the professor was standing. The guide shook his head in agreement.

The professor continued: "We were in such a hurry, we did not even see this passageway."

He took a couple of steps into the newly discovered tunnel. The new passageway ran in an upward direction, so no water from Hans River flowed into it. The professor looked around. Then he placed his nose to the ground again. He had been right! In the dry dirt and rock of this passageway, he smelled only Axel's trail. Then he turned his attention from the ground to the wall of the entrance. He leaped up and placed his front paws onto the right side of the entrance. His lamp shone on granite formations— just like the kind his nephew had been closely studying the last time they had seen him.

Professor Lidenbrock poked his head farther into the tunnel's entrance. "Axel!" he yelled. "Axel! Can you hear me?" He waited for a reply, but there was only silence. The professor turned to Hans. "Prepare to fire another shot."

The professor turned back to look into the cavern. Then, with all his might, he listened very carefully. An idea struck him.

"Axel!" Professor Lidenbrock called for his nephew once more. Then he pressed his right ear against the cool granite wall and listened. Very faintly, he heard a reply.

"Uncle Lidenbrock . . ." Axel replied.

"Axel, my boy, is that you?" the professor replied, his ear still pressed against the wall.

There was a short delay between his question and Axel's answer. "Yes, yes!" replied Axel.

"Where are you?" the professor asked.

There was a pause. Then Axel replied, "I'm lost in total darkness! I fell and broke my lamp." Another pause. "But where are you, Uncle? I can barely hear you!"

"Speak into the wall!" replied the professor. "The granite carries the sound of your voice, like wire conducts electricity. Keep talking and we'll find you!" Professor Lidenbrock turned to Hans, who was slinging his rifle over his shoulder. "Let us hurry, Hans."

Slowly, the professor and Hans made their way through the newly discovered tunnel. The sound of Hans River faded away behind them.

Axel continued to speak. "When I first heard your voice, Uncle, I thought I was losing my mind and just imagining I heard you."

"Keep your courage, dear Axel," the professor answered, speaking directly into the solid rock wall. "We shall soon be together again."

But while Axel was making his last remark, the

73

professor thought he heard footsteps. It seemed as if Axel had been walking.

"Axel!" the professor called out. "Stay right where you are! It is too dangerous for you to be moving around without the aid of light. Don't worry. *We* will find *you*."

A pause. Then: "It's all right, Uncle. I can feel my way along the wall. With both of us moving steadily toward each other, we will be together in half the time!"

The professor was quite worried. "Making up time is not worth any injuries you could suffer by groping about in total darkness." He put his mouth even closer to the granite wall. "So please, Axel, stay where you—"

Suddenly, Professor Lidenbrock heard a terrible noise. It was the sound of falling rock.

"Uncle!" Axel's voice came through the tunnel. There were some more crumbling noises, then only silence.

"Axel!" the professor cried. He put his ear to the wall and waited for an answer. When none came, he repeated his cry. "Axel! Axel!"

He waited, his ear pressed hard to the granite wall. Axel did not answer.

Professor Lidenbrock turned to Hans. "Hans, I fear that Axel has met with a horrible accident. We must now double our efforts to find him!"

Once again, the professor placed his nose to the ground. He picked up Axel's trail. He and Hans would have to rely on only one of his senses to find Axel. The professor hoped it wouldn't be too late!

Oh, I hate to leave a good story during such a tense moment! But my stomach is telling me that something else is late. My dinnertime!

Chapter Seven

Wishbone placed his front paws against the kitchen countertop. He breathed in the delicious aroma of freshly chopped vegetables. His stomach growled as he looked around the kitchen. Maybe he could locate a snack before dinner. Trying to figure out the mysteries of the golden disk was fun, but even great detectives stopped their investigations to take a dinner break.

Wishbone turned back to the vegetables. His stomach growled once more. That was it! *Gold or no gold, new chew toys or just old slobbery ones, this dog has to eat!*

Wishbone decided to take a break in his waiting for dinner. He trotted into the living room. There he found Joe, Sam, and David, their heads buried in library books at the coffee table. "Okay, people," he barked, "how about a dinner break?" Everyone kept reading. From upstairs, Wishbone heard a door shut. Then he heard Ellen's footsteps as she walked down the stairs. *Finally!* he thought. *Ellen will save us from starving!*

Wishbone ran to the foot of the stairs to meet Ellen. "Hey, Ellen," he said, "wouldn't you say it was time for something? I'll give you a hint. It rhymes with 'winter dime,' 'bitter lime,' and 'winner mime'!"

He gave a small bark as Ellen came down the last few steps, but she didn't notice him. She was thumbing through the book she was carrying as she got down the last step and headed for the living room.

"Dinner time!" Wishbone said, as he sat up, trying to get Ellen's attention. *"That's* what time it is!" It was no use. He let out a sigh and walked sadly into the living room to join the others.

"I found my old Latin dictionary," Ellen told the kids. She pulled a chair close to the book-covered coffee table and sat down.

"Great!" David replied. "We got lots of books from the library, but we haven't found anything helpful yet."

Wishbone tried a different approach. He walked over to Sam and wagged his tail. "Hey, guys, food's almost ready!"

Sam gave Wishbone a quick scratch. "You know," she said, looking through a book, "maybe it's a Roman coin."

I wonder how you say "Come and get it" in Latin, Wishbone thought.

Joe looked up from the book he was reading. "I don't think there were ever any Romans in Oakdale," he said with a small smile.

Ellen held the gold disk up to the light. She looked back and forth from the object to her Latin dictionary. Then she picked up a pen and wrote down something on a piece of paper. "It's not a coin," she announced. She held out the small disk to the kids. "It's a medal."

"A medal?" David asked.

Ellen examined the disk even more closely. "I think so. There's a date on it—1864." She placed the medal on the table. "That should give us more of a clue."

"How?" Sam asked, looking up from her book.

"Well, let's think about it," she said, as everyone looked up from their book. "What was going on back then?"

Wishbone walked over to Ellen and rested his head against her leg. "People were eating dinner!"

"Well," Sam began, "lots of railroads were being built."

Wishbone went over to Sam and nudged her hand with his nose. "And they were eating lots of dinners."

"There was the gold rush out west," Joe added.

Wishbone moved from Sam to Joe. "And the prospectors always stopped their work to eat dinner!"

David chimed in, "Don't forget the Civil War."

Ellen put down the pen as she finished writing. "Of course!" she exclaimed.

"Yes!" Wishbone replied with a bark. "Lots of soldiers eating dinner!"

Ellen continued. "Okay, here it is." She closed her Latin dictionary and read from the piece of paper she had been writing on. "'A decoration for the sake of honor, for military bravery and' . . . That is all there is."

David picked up the golden disk. He looked at it with a new sense of wonder. "It must be a medal that was given to a soldier. Maybe it belonged to someone who fought in the Civil War!"

"The Civil War," Joe said to himself. An idea came to him. He pulled a book out from under one of the stacks on the coffee table, placed it on his lap, and flipped it open.

Wishbone walked in front of the table and lay down. It seemed that the conversation had gotten way too serious for anyone to remember dinner. *I guess I'll just lie here and try to look really sad—the action of a starving dog.*

Ellen said, "Whoever received the medal must have been some kind of hero."

David handed the medal to Sam. "Is that this 'N. J.' person?" she asked.

"I'm not sure," Ellen replied.

"Hey, can I see it for a minute?" Joe said, his face still buried in the book he was reading.

Wishbone's ears perked up as he heard the excitement in Joe's voice. He got up and walked over to Joe as Sam handed him the medal. Joe looked closely at the medal, then back at the book. He turned the page, then placed the medal onto the page. Wishbone placed his front paws on Joe's legs to raise himself up and get a better look. On the page, he saw pictures of a couple of different medals.

"This book is a catalogue of American medals and honors," he said to his mother and friends. "Maybe there's a match for it in the Civil War section." He picked up the medal and turned another page as everyone gathered closely.

Finally—a light at the end of the tunnel! Wishbone thought. *And maybe that light is a heat lamp, keeping dinner nice and warm.*

"Here it is!" Joe's exclamation knocked Wishbone out of his dinner daydream. The little dog looked at the book. He saw Joe holding the medal next to a picture of a medal on the book page.

"I can't believe we found it!" Sam said excitedly.

"'The Courageous Service Award,'" Joe said, as he read the caption under the picture. "'Limited to the USCT.'"

"What does 'USCT' stand for?" Sam asked.

"Whatever it stands for," David answered, as he looked at the book, "it says it's limited. That means not many of them were given out. I bet it's more valuable than we thought!"

"Too bad we don't have the backing piece," Ellen said, picking up the medal.

"What do you mean?" Joe asked.

"Well, the inscription stops in mid-sentence," Ellen said. "It must continue on the other side."

A smile brightened Sam's face. "And that's why the other side is plain."

"The backing piece of the medal must have fallen off," David said.

Wishbone perked up. He could feel the excitement level rising in the living room. Unfortunately, he knew it had nothing to do with dinner.

Ellen turned the mysterious medal over in her hand. "Well, if you can find the backing, you'll probably know who 'N. J.' is."

The kids looked at one another. Each said at once, "The hole!" Joe, Sam, and David put down their books and headed for the front door. Ellen held the medal tightly and followed them outside.

Well, it looks as if dinner will have to wait! Just like Professor Lidenbrock's journey to the center of the Earth, this Oakdale adventure is far from over!

Chapter Eight

Professor Lidenbrock watched with concern as Axel struggled to regain consciousness. He was lying on the ground, covered with a blanket. A bandage was wrapped around his head. There was a small spot of blood seeping through just above his left eye. They were inside a small opening surrounded by several large rocks. The professor placed one paw onto his nephew's arm when he saw him move. Axel slowly opened his eyes.

"He lives! He lives!" the professor exclaimed.

"Yes, my good uncle," Axel whispered.

Professor Lidenbrock's tail wagged. "My dear boy," he said, "you are saved!"

Hans looked over the professor's shoulder. *"God-dag,"* he said quickly. Then he left the small area of circled boulders.

"Good day, Hans, good day," Axel called after him in a stronger voice. The professor watched Axel as he looked around. The different surroundings seemed to confuse him. "What happened, Uncle?" Axel asked.

"After you were separated from Hans and me," Professor Lidenbrock said, "you must have fallen down a shaft in the tunnel. When Hans and I found you, you had an injury to your head. You've been unconscious for a whole day. Even though Hans picked you up and carried you here, I feared you might never wake up." The professor placed a paw on Axel's chest. "I thought I might lose you, dear nephew. No journey is worth that."

Axel smiled as he placed a hand on his uncle's paw. His attention then shifted to his surroundings. "Uncle," he began, "I see no lamp lit and no torch burning."

"This is true," the professor answered. His excitement grew as he gazed around the bright area.

Axel continued. "Yet, everything is bright."

"Yes," the professor said, his tail beginning to wag.

"And, Uncle," Axel said, as he began to sit up, "I'm sure I can hear a low murmur, like the washing of waves upon sand."

The professor's tail wagged with more force. It was very difficult for him to keep from telling Axel where they were. But he was determined for Axel to enjoy the discovery, just the way he and Hans had.

Axel spoke again. "Uncle, I do believe I can hear the sighing of the wind."

"Yes," the professor answered. "All of what you say is true."

A concerned look made Axel's face tighten. He touched the bandage on his head. "It is my opinion that my head is not exactly right. In fact, I do believe myself slightly delirious."

Trying to hold back laughter, the professor replied, "Axel, dear boy, you are not delirious."

"Then, Uncle," Axel asked, "did we return to the surface of the Earth?"

"Certainly not," the professor replied, surprised by the question.

"How, then, do you explain all of these things?" his nephew asked.

"I will not even try to explain," Professor Lidenbrock said. "The whole matter is completely unexplainable." He turned and began to trot toward a place where there was an opening in the group of large boulders that almost completely surrounded them. "Come, Axel. You shall judge for yourself."

Axel rose. Placing his hand on one of the boulders for support, he slowly followed his uncle.

The professor said, "You will then find that geological science still holds many mysteries, and we are going to educate the world!"

As the professor stepped out from behind the boulders, he turned back to watch Axel's expression. His nephew came out, and the bright light made him squint. After a few seconds, his eyes widened at what he saw.

The professor followed his nephew's gaze. "Axel, dear boy, you are looking at the Central Sea!"

Professor Lidenbrock's tail wagged as if he were viewing the scene for the first time. They were in a huge cavern. The size was impossible to calculate. A vast, limitless sea of water spread out before them for miles. Its waves gently broke against a shore of golden sand. On each side of them, the shoreline disappeared into the hazy distance. Above them, a mighty mountain of rock rose miles into the air. The ceiling of the enormous underground cavern was blocked from view by clouds. Each of those clouds was filled with electrical currents. Silent lightning bolts twisted with one another and shot back and forth across the artificial sky. The action created a very crisp white light that completely lit up the entire cavern. This electric light did not give off the warmth that sunlight provided.

The wind that was created out of this unique atmospheric condition gently blew across the sea. It sent a dash of spray onto the professor's muzzle. He licked off the salty moisture and took in a deep breath. The air had a fresh saltiness, along with a slightly electrical scent, as well. No doubt it came from the ozone created by the electrical discharges above.

"Well," the professor said, turning back to Axel, "do you feel strong enough for a walk down the beach?"

"Certainly," Axel replied. "Nothing would give me greater pleasure."

"Well then, my boy," Professor Lidenbrock said, "let us go for a walk!"

They turned to their left and began to walk along the shore. Hans stayed behind to make camp. Although the professor was the most excited about their underground journey, he did get a certain feeling of comfort from walking in what seemed to be the open air. *It's nice to have the sea air ruffling your fur sometimes.*

The professor and his nephew traveled down the sea's coast. They discussed the different rock formations. They also talked about the possible effect that the Earth's moon had on the tides of a body of water that flowed so deep beneath the surface. The landscape didn't change much until they reached a large indentation in the cavern's wall. In that spot, they discovered a very unusual forest.

The strange trees were very tall, smooth, and completely without leaves. The only thing keeping them from being mere poles were the flat, round disk shapes on top of them. To Professor Lidenbrock, they looked like umbrellas.

The professor trotted over to get a better look. Axel followed. As they went into the forest and walked under the shade cast by the odd-looking trees, the temperature dropped dramatically. There were thousands of these forty-foot-high trees!

As the professor got close to one of the trees, he turned to see Axel rubbing his hand along one of the trunks. His hand moved smoothly over the surface. This was not the bark of a tree. The professor turned back to give a sniff to the tree nearest him. A familiar smell came from these towering giants, but the professor couldn't put his paw on what it was. He looked up. Then, from what he saw, the answer came to him.

"Axel!" he said with excitement. "Look up, and these mysterious trees will be explained." Axel looked up, and a smile came to his face. "Do you see the ribbed shape?" the professor asked him.

"Yes, Uncle," Axel replied. "Could these really be . . ."

The professor finished his thought: ". . . giant mushrooms."

Just as the professor had expected, there seemed to be no end to the fascinating discoveries to be made miles

beneath the Earth's surface. He put his nose against the stem of the giant mushroom once more and took in a deep breath. *There would have to be a pretty big pot for the amount of spaghetti sauce it would take to hold one of these mushrooms.*

As Professor Lidenbrock was enjoying the strong mushroom aroma, another scent crept into his nostrils. This, too, was a familiar smell. It was pulling him, ever so welcomingly, to the source. As if he were in a trance, the professor left Axel to examine the mushroom forest. In doing so, he slowly walked back toward the beach.

He finally reached the beach, then raised his nose high into the air. The professor sniffed, then turned left toward a small hill. His paws sank a bit into the ground as he climbed the low sand dune. When he reached the top, he saw the source of the enchanting scent. In front of him, lying scattered on the beach, was a huge collection of . . . bones!

The professor ran down the side of the dune and dove right into the middle of the bone pile. There were all kinds of bones! Big bones! Little bones! Bones with rough edges! Bones with smooth edges! Bones with big round knobs at the ends. *Ones so big that you have to open your mouth really wide to chew! And you can't even chew them—you just scrape your teeth down the sides!*

"Uncle?"

The professor looked up to see his nephew standing on top of the sand dune. He then realized he was lying on top of a pile of bones. The professor had one end of a very large bone resting between his front paws, and the other end resting in his mouth.

"Uh . . . yes, Axel?" the professor said. "Look! Another amazing discovery!"

Axel's eyes moved from his uncle to the bones that were lying around him. He slowly made his way down the dune and to his uncle. "Uncle," he said as he reached down and picked up the bone the professor was chewing. "You have discovered the lower jaw bone of a mastodon— a creature similar to a giant ancient elephant."

"I have?" the professor asked. He shook his head. For a brief moment he had lost control of his emotions. "Yes, I have," he said, fully recovered. "There was quite a variety of prehistoric animals that lived and died on these shores."

"But how can there have been such beasts living in granite caverns?" Axel asked.

"That fact can be explained both simply and geologically," the professor said. "It is very possible that above ground many earthquakes took place in ancient times. When the ground opened up, large amounts of soil, along with anything on them, were thrown deep into the Earth."

"But, Uncle," Axel asked, "if these ancient animals survived and used to live in these underground regions, is it possible that one of these huge monsters may, at this very moment now, be still hiding behind one of those mighty rocks over there?"

Professor Lidenbrock looked in the direction of the boulders. Then he turned back to face Axel. "Don't worry, dear boy," he said. "It is my strong belief that we are the only animals here today." Axel still stood at the top of the dune. "Come, Axel. We should leave." The professor started to walk up the dune. Then he quickly backtracked to grab a small bone in his mouth. Finally, he returned to the top of the dune. *Hey, it never hurts to collect samples,* he thought.

Together, Axel and Professor Lidenbrock walked quietly back toward their camp. The professor looked around their strange new surroundings. He wondered what the great Saknussemm had thought when he had first set foot in this gigantic cavern.

As if to answer the professor's question, a slight breeze blew over his fur. His tail slowly moved back and forth as a feeling of great satisfaction and triumph washed over him. He knew that Arne Saknussemm would have been proud of what the three travelers had accomplished so far.

The silence between uncle and nephew was finally broken when Axel spoke. "So, Uncle," he said. "We have made a great discovery."

"A great discovery, indeed," the professor replied.

Axel continued: "So, what are your plans for the future? Are you thinking of getting back to the surface of our beautiful Earth?"

Professor Lidenbrock stopped walking and turned to Axel. "Certainly not!" he exclaimed. "You are surely not thinking of doing anything so silly?" He didn't give his nephew a chance to answer. Instead, he started to walk again. "My plan is to go forward and continue our amazing journey. We have been very lucky, and in the future I hope we shall be even more so."

"But," Axel began as he followed his uncle, "how are we to cross this huge underground sea?"

"It is not my plan to swim across it," the professor said. "We will, however, leave our camp tomorrow."

"What!" This time Axel was the first to stop. "We are about to cross an unknown sea. Where, if I may ask, is the ship to carry us?"

The professor stopped. With his head tilted slightly, he looked directly at Axel. "Well, my dear boy, it will not be exactly what you would call a ship." He looked out upon the sea. "For the moment, we must be content and build a good, solid raft."

Axel almost laughed at the idea. "*A raft?* Down here, a raft is as impossible to build as a ship," he said, raising both hands in the air. "I am at a total loss to imagine—"

The professor didn't let his nephew finish. "My good Axel, if you were to listen instead of talking so much, you would hear," he said a bit impatiently.

Axel stopped talking. From the look on Axel's face, the professor could tell that his nephew was now beginning to hear what he himself had been hearing for quite some time already. In the distance, and when the wind blew a certain way, the faint sounds of a hammer hitting wood could be heard.

"That sound . . ." Axel began.

". . . is the sound of Hans building a raft," the professor finished. "He has been at work for many hours." Professor Lidenbrock turned and trotted toward the hammering sounds. He heard the gritty shuffling of feet in sand. He knew Axel was, once again, following him.

"But where has he found wood to build a raft?" Axel asked.

"Follow me, dear nephew," the professor said, "and all will be understood."

They walked along the beach for fifteen minutes. The hammering sound increased in volume with every step. They passed the small area where Axel had spent time recovering from his accident. Finally, they climbed a small dune. They reached the top of the rise. Spread out before them was a great number of tree limbs—joints and bows—enough to build a fleet of rafts. In the middle, they saw Hans hard at work on a half-finished raft made from the scattered wood.

Axel stared in amazement. Then he asked, "Where did all this wood come from?"

The professor ran down the slope. "It is mostly fossil wood," he answered.

Axel hurried down the dune behind the professor. "But, Uncle," he said, "it must be as hard and heavy as iron. Therefore, it will certainly not float."

"That would be the case," the professor replied, as he trotted over and around the many trunks. "Many of these pieces have become fossils. But others have not yet undergone the change to fossil form." He walked over to a very small branch and sniffed it. "But, then again," the professor added, "there is no proof like a demonstration."

He picked up the branch. With a quick jerk, he tossed the branch into the nearby sea. The piece of wood, after having disappeared under a wave for a moment, came to the surface. It floated with the rhythmic motion created by the wind and tide.

The professor began to climb up the dune. When he reached the top, he turned back to Axel. "Come, dear boy," he said in a gentle voice. "No doubt your injuries have made you tired and hungry." He then looked out over what he had named the Central Sea. The wind gently stroked his fur and blew the pleasing odor of the salty water into his nostrils. He kept his gaze on the horizon but continued to speak to Axel. "You must prepare yourself." Then he added, "We must all prepare ourselves, for our incredible journey is not over yet."

The professor and Axel then headed back to the small cave where their supplies were stored.

Chapter Nine

The next evening, thanks to the hard work and talent of Hans, the raft was finished. It was about ten feet long and five feet wide. The planks, bound together with strong ropes, were solid and firm. Once the craft had been placed into the water, it floated calmly upon the sea. It had a mast made of two pieces of wood fastened together. From the mast, a sail made from a linen sheet flapped gracefully in the wind.

Hans worked the rudder. Professor Lidenbrock and Axel sat near the center of the raft, where all of their gear was tightly strapped down. The professor was delighted that a strong and constant wind blew the tiny raft across the underground sea at a fast pace. He turned back for a moment and saw the shore they had launched from slowly disappear into the distance.

Professor Lidenbrock looked at Axel and said, "We have a beautiful breeze and a splendid sea. We are moving quickly. I believe this sea to be no more than one hundred and fifty miles long." He looked out to the vast horizon. "If I am correct, it will not be too long until we see land." The professor was eager to reach land and to descend once again.

For two days they sailed the Central Sea. No sign of land lay anywhere. Professor Lidenbrock, however, knew they weren't in any danger. Before they left on their journey, they had filled their canteens in the various fresh-water streams that they found flowing from the granite walls of the cavern near their camp. Food wasn't a problem, either. Hans had even been successful in catching some fish.

With a hook and line, the skilled guide had pulled up a number of strange fish. They were fish the professor immediately recognized. However, until that moment, he had only viewed the creatures in books, and as old fossils he had studied in the past. Amazingly, all the fish that Hans caught with his simple fishing gear had been extinct for millions of years.

The ancient fish had something else in common with one another, as well. They were all blind. Like many other kinds of fish that lived in dark, underground waters, they had no need to see. The discovery of the mutant fish provided the professor's journey with very important scientific knowledge. The bizarre creatures also were an excellent source of food for the long sea voyage of the three travelers. The new, plentiful food supply seemed to put everyone at ease. Even Axel seemed to be enjoying the smooth sailing.

The professor had underestimated just how large the sea was. They had entered the shaft twenty-five days ago and had traveled almost one hundred miles below the Earth's surface. At the moment, though, they weren't going down any farther. Also, they weren't making any progress with their scientific discoveries.

The professor thought all of this time spent sailing

was a complete waste. He hadn't gone so far away from his home to take a pleasure cruise! The voyage on a raft through an empty sea started to annoy him and make him grow restless. What troubled him even more was the fact that they might not even be following Saknussemm's trail anymore.

Professor Lidenbrock lay down on his back. Perhaps the sea cruise would pass by more quickly if he took a nap. The professor stared toward the top of the giant cavern. The electrical charges danced hypnotically over and through the clouds. Sometimes, the three travelers had seen a few of the blue-white streaks shoot down from the clouds and strike the water's surface.

The lightning holds little danger, the professor thought. *The chances of a lightning bolt striking a small raft as it sails along on a large underground ocean are probably a million to one.*

The professor's eyelids began to droop. He was slowly being rocked to sleep by the raft's lazy movement on the water. The light show above seemed to add to his feeling of relaxation. He watched the electric vines quickly branch across the clouds. In one part of the sky, several strands of bright lightning began to swirl into a tiny hypnotic ball. Their circular motion went faster and faster.

"Fascinating," the professor said sleepily. He watched the ball spin, then fall sharply away from the clouds. It was as if the ball of electric strands had suddenly gained too much weight to float among the clouds. "Wonderful," Professor Lidenbrock mumbled. He was almost asleep. "Now we can get a closer look."

The professor shook his head awake. He suddenly leaped to all four paws.

"A closer look?" he asked himself in surprise. He stared at the falling ball of lightning. The tiny circle appeared as if it was going to plunge into the water only about twenty-five feet from the raft. It zigzagged unevenly as it made its way down. When it finally came close to the water's surface, the ball stopped. It hovered briefly about three feet from the waves. Tiny sparks of electricity reached out in every direction. Then, suddenly, the electric ball quickly made its way toward the raft.

"Uncle," Axel said from the front of the raft.

"I see it," Professor Lidenbrock replied.

The fiery ball slowed as it reached the raft. Yet Axel still had to duck to keep from being hit by it. With a loud crackling sound, the bright ball made its way toward Hans and the back of the raft. It slowed and seemed to inspect the raft as it reached out with long, thin sparks. It was as if the object was feeling everything with tiny blue-white fingers.

The ball floated and bobbed in front of Hans. Then it started to go back in the direction from which it had come. The professor had to step to the side of the raft as it passed him and aimed toward the center of the craft. Professor Lidenbrock let out a strong cough. The harsh fumes that came from the sphere made it difficult for him to breathe.

The electric globe continued to reach out and touch everything on the raft. It acted as if it was inspecting all of the travelers' supplies. More tiny ribbons of electricity moved over their knapsacks. It quickly made its way around the piles of supplies and went toward their small leather pouch of gunpowder.

Professor Lidenbrock backed away from the threatening ball and prepared for a terrible explosion. If even one single spark touched the gunpowder, then the entire pouch would explode and also put an end to the raft and its three passengers.

Luckily, however, the powder did not explode. Instead of touching the pouch, the ball of sparks rose high in the air. It floated above the three travelers, its electric arms reaching out farther than ever. Then, suddenly, it exploded in an amazing flash of light. Professor Lidenbrock shielded his eyes with one paw.

The bizarre ball of electricity had disappeared completely. The only electricity that remained was what danced in the clouds high above. The professor looked up toward the cavern's ceiling. He now felt that the odds of being struck by lightning were just a little bit higher than he had thought before.

It took a couple of hours for the three explorers to calm down after their unexpected meeting with the ball of electricity. There was no way the professor could sleep after that close call. Instead, he tried to take his mind off the long journey by running some more scientific tests.

"Axel," the professor said to his nephew, "tie one of the crowbars securely to the end of our longest rope." He watched as his nephew followed the instructions. When he was finished, he placed the bound crowbar and coil of rope in front of his uncle.

The professor then took the other end of the rope in his mouth. With his nose, he edged the crowbar into the water. He watched as the rope quickly unwound from the round coil of rope. When almost all of the rope was lowered under the water's surface, the professor moved to the center of the raft and braced himself. The rope in his mouth pulled tight with a quick jerk. This disappointed the professor very much. Being a scientist, he wanted to record all the information about the sea. He didn't know how wide it was yet. Since the crowbar hadn't seemed to hit the bottom of the sea, the professor didn't know how deep it was, either.

Professor Lidenbrock sighed. He stepped over to the edge of the raft. He placed a paw on the rope to hold it steady. Then he released his grip from the end. He moved his mouth farther along the rope and clasped his teeth onto the part closest to the water. Then he lifted his paw and pulled the rope back onto the raft with his mouth. As he was moving back to the center of the raft, the line suddenly became heavier and harder to pull in.

"Akthel, Hans," the professor said through clenched teeth, "lend me a hand vith thiss line."

Axel and Hans quickly helped the professor. They pulled hard on the slowly moving rope until the crowbar finally broke through the water's surface. The professor walked over to Axel as he picked up the crowbar. Axel ran his fingers over what seemed to be several large dents made in the iron bar's surface.

"Tander," Hans said, leaning over Axel's shoulder.

Axel turned to look at the professor. The frown on Axel's face showed he was waiting for a translation.

"'Teeth,'" said the professor, in the same quick, flat way that Hans had spoken. Then, what he had just translated hit him full force. *Teeth? Making dents like that in a solid iron bar? What kind of giant beast could have made those marks?*

The professor went over to get a close look. He gave the crowbar a sniff. Then he carefully studied the grooves. He slowly looked up at Axel and Hans. They, in turn, looked at him and each other. There was a long silence.

Boom!!!!

The raft rose completely out of the water with a sudden jolt! It floated in midair for a moment, then slammed back onto the sea's surface! Professor Lidenbrock dug his claws into the raft, trying not to be thrown overboard. He saw that Axel and Hans were also struggling to stay aboard.

"What is it?" Axel yelled, a strong tone of terror in his voice.

Hans raised his hand and pointed. Both the professor and Axel followed his gaze. They saw a huge, shiny black mass moving away from the raft. Atop the mass, a giant fin sliced through the water's surface.

"It is a colossal monster!" Axel cried.

At that moment, the creature's enormous head surfaced about fifty yards in front of its huge body. Rows of gigantic teeth glistened as its long, dolphinlike mouth gaped wide open. An eye, as big as a human's head, slowly surfaced and blazed wildly in the cavern's electric glow.

The professor recognized the horrifying creature at once. "It is the most fearful of all of the ancient reptiles!" the professor yelled. The roar of the splashing water created by the creature almost drowned out his voice. "It is the world-famous ichthyosaurus, or great fish lizard." He turned to Hans, who was already making his way back to the rudder. "Hans, we must get away from this terrible beast!"

The three travelers rode through the great current that the creature's enormous tail had created. Hans used the rudder as a paddle and quickly turned the raft around. Professor Lidenbrock and Axel watched the ichthyosaurus as it turned around as well. It began to make its way toward their tiny raft. The beast looked like a hideous porpoise the size of a whale. Its shiny black skin glistened under the electricity above.

Suddenly, the professor heard another roar of gushing water behind him. He turned to face the front of the raft. He saw another giant's head rise from the water. This time, there was no body behind it—only a single head the size of three of their rafts put together. Water flowed off the scaly head as it quietly floated there in front of them. With its mouth closed, its giant eyes stared at them as the raft headed straight for it. From where the travelers were, all the creature would have to do was open its mouth, and the raft and its passengers would sail right in.

The second creature did open its mouth. But instead of swallowing the travelers whole, it let out a deafening roar. The smell of rotting fish filled the air as the monster's breath blew over them like the fierce wind from a hurricane. Then the head rose out of the water, revealing a long, scaly neck. The creature's neck kept rising and rising. Finally, it towered above the raft like a mighty tree. At last its giant body rose behind it from the water, and four enormous fins splashed on all sides of it. The professor was then able to identify this creature as a plesiosaurus—an immense marine reptile from the Jurassic era, about 190 million years ago!

Hans stopped paddling. He removed his rifle from around his shoulder. The professor knew, however, that the lead ball from a gun would have little effect on the thick, scaly armor of this creature.

Professor Lidenbrock turned to the rear of the raft. There, he saw the ichthyosaurus closing in on the raft. Its mouth was opened wide to receive its dinner. Then the professor turned and looked high above them to the plesiosaurus doing the same. Its long neck bent as its open mouth came rushing toward the raft.

So this is how the adventure will end, the professor thought. *There is still much to discover. Now we are doomed to be torn to pieces and swallowed by two ancient dinosaurs.*

The professor looked back and saw that Axel now had the rifle. Hans was quickly paddling the boat from between the two giant sea creatures. However, they were much too fast and too large to outrun.

Professor Lidenbrock looked back toward the oncoming attackers. He expected they would change their course of attack as the raft drifted away from the two. Instead, both creatures continued to swim in the same direction—toward each other! They weren't after the tiny, meaningless raft. They were attacking *each other!*

The plesiosaurus lunged at the ichthyosaurus. Its long, whiplike neck pushed its head down upon its foe with an amazing speed for such a large creature. Its open mouth locked onto the ichthyosaurus's neck. The large, dolphinlike creature rolled in defense. It pulled its long-necked attacker toward it like a giant spool rolling in thread. Finally, the plesiosaurus released its grip, backed off, and circled around for another attack.

Professor Lidenbrock could not believe what they were witnessing. The enormous animals attacked each other with incredible fury. Such a fight had probably never been seen before by human eyes. The sea beasts raised mountains of water, which dashed spray over the raft as it was tossed to and fro by the waves. Hideous hisses and fierce roars seemed to shake the gloomy granite roof of the huge cavern as the deadly warriors held each other in a tight grip.

Several times, the professor expected the raft to be overturned and thrown headlong under the waves. As if

in the midst of a horrible storm, Hans lowered the sail and manned the rudder. He tried desperately to steer them away from the swirling waters.

Often, as the creatures chased each other far away from the raft, it seemed as if the battle would leave them altogether. But just as they had left, the two ancient dinosaurs would make their way back toward the tiny raft to toss it around once more in their wake.

Then, as quickly as the chaos had begun, it was over. The ichthyosaurus and the plesiosaurus disappeared beneath the waves. Behind them, they left a rough and choppy sea. Their departure came so quickly that the travelers' raft was nearly sucked down in the whirlpool the beasts had created.

As the sea began to calm, Professor Lidenbrock looked at Axel and Hans. Hans had stopped paddling. Now he scanned the horizon, and Axel did the same. The professor turned his gaze back to the now calm sea. Except for a small ringing left in his ears from the monsters' roar, all was silent. It seemed that the last part of the terrible war between the prehistoric creatures would take place in the depths of the sea, with no one to watch.

The professor looked at Axel and Hans. "Come, Hans," the professor said, his voice calm and relaxed. "Let us leave this place. I don't wish to be around when the winner of the battle returns."

Hans handled the rudder. Axel set down the rifle and raised the sail. Professor Lidenbrock looked back as they continued their journey. He was glad the sea battle was over, but he was also happy it had taken place. No one had probably ever witnessed what they did that day. And even though he wouldn't trade that memory for anything, the professor decided not to take any more depth measurements for the rest of their sea voyage.

After another day of sailing, the three travelers began to hear a strange noise. It sounded like water crashing against some unknown shore. That wouldn't have been strange—if there had been a shoreline nearby. But after Hans had climbed to the top of the mast to investigate, he saw absolutely no sign of land.

"Curious sound," the professor said.

"What if it is a mighty waterfall?" Axel asked. "What if we sail over its edge and into a deep hole?"

"Then at least we will be moving forward on our journey to the center of the Earth," the professor replied, his tail wagging. "Don't worry, dear nephew," the professor continued. "I don't believe the sound comes from such a waterfall." At least, the professor *hoped* it didn't.

As they sailed on, the strange sound grew louder. Once again, Hans climbed the mast and scanned the horizon.

"*Der nere!*" the Icelander cried. He pointed in the distance, then returned to the base of the raft.

The professor and Axel turned toward the direction where Hans had pointed. The professor's sharp eyesight pinpointed what their guide had seen. "There," he told his nephew. "A tremendous spurt of water rises out of the waves in the distance."

"Another ancient monster?" Axel replied. "Let us steer away from it!"

Professor Lidenbrock stared at the giant water spout a little longer. He wondered what kind of beast could fill itself with so much water. "Let us remain on our present course. I wish to take a closer look," he announced. He could tell that Axel was not pleased by the idea of being close to another giant sea creature. The professor, how-ever, wanted to study the odd phenomenon.

As the tiny raft sailed closer, the sound of the rushing water got louder. The giant spout of liquid seemed to grow, as well. It began to tower over the three explorers, reaching a height of five hundred feet. As they approached, they also noticed something else. Under the water's spout stretched a long, black, enormous body of some kind. It sat directly on top of the water like a dark, mysterious island.

Professor Lidenbrock remembered hearing stories of sailors who had stepped from their ships onto the backs of giant sleeping whales, mistaking them for land. Could that be the case with *this* dark mass? If it *was* another sea creature, it was lying motionless. It was also ten times as large as the other monsters the travelers had seen earlier.

"We mustn't go any closer!" Axel cried.

The professor could hear the fear in his nephew's voice. "Calm yourself, Axel," the professor said.

"This is insane, Uncle!" Axel replied. "A creature this size can swallow us whole!"

Professor Lidenbrock had to admit that he, too, felt a sense of fear beginning to make a knot inside his own stomach.

They sailed a bit closer and, once again, Hans pointed toward the menacing object. *"Holme!"* he said.

"An island!" the professor translated. "Yes, of course it is!" The professor's tail wagged wildly.

"But what about the water spout?" Axel asked.

"Geyser," said Hans.

The professor laughed. "Of course—it's a geyser!" Professor Lidenbrock barked with delight. "A geyser—just like those found all over Iceland!"

All three travelers laughed as they sailed past the

forbidding-looking island. The professor was very amused that they could be so easily fooled. Then, again, with everything that they had experienced so far, he felt anything was possible.

Chapter Ten

The sturdy raft sailed across the Central Sea for two more days before the travelers reached land. When the three travelers finally brought their craft ashore, Axel checked on their supplies and equipment. Many were lost overboard during the terrible struggle between the two ancient beasts. Hans made repairs to the raft, for they didn't know if this was the right port in which to continue following Saknussemm's trail. Professor Lidenbrock looked over the new land. He was thrilled to have his paws on solid ground. It felt good to be off what seemed to be a never-ending sea.

Professor Lidenbrock did recalculate, however, the Central Sea's size. It was more than eighteen hundred miles, wider than Europe's Mediterranean Sea. And that was just the distance that they had crossed. For all they knew, the mysterious sea that lay underneath the Earth's crust could be as much as ten times that in length. Either way, the professor hoped they wouldn't find that out.

His calculations completed, Professor Lidenbrock watched as Axel finished making his check of their supplies. "Well, Axel," the professor called to his nephew, "what do we have left?"

Axel looked up to his uncle from the beach below, where he had laid out their supplies. Then he walked up the small hill to where his uncle stood. "We have four months' worth of food and water," Axel answered. Then he added, "That's if we use everything carefully."

"Four months!" cried the professor with glee. "Then we shall have plenty of time to complete our journey." He reared onto his hind legs for a moment. "With what will be left over, I plan to give a grand dinner to my two traveling partners when we return!"

Professor Lidenbrock then turned his back to the sea. He raised his muzzle and sniffed the slight breeze blowing across the hills. The land that they had reached looked very much like the land where their sea voyage had begun. Scary-looking cliffs rose to meet a high granite ceiling above. And on each side of them, the beach stretched way into the distance. Eventually, it was swallowed by a distant fog created by a combination of sea spray and low-lying underground clouds.

The professor turned back to face Axel. "Come, dear nephew," he said. "While Hans repairs the raft, let us go on a journey of discovery. We shall see if we are still on the great Saknussemm's path!"

The professor and Axel walked along the beach, their feet and paws crunching over shells of every shape and size. There was evidence of sea life from every period of creation stretched along the shore and in the neighboring dunes. They even discovered empty giant turtle shells. One was so huge that the professor was easily able to walk into the center of it. Its former inhabitant had long since passed on to take its place with the rest of the extinct species.

The remains of ancient, or not-so-ancient, sea life were only part of what was to be found in this new area. After walking about a mile along the shore, the pair came across another huge field of bones! Once again, every species in the history of animal life seemed to be represented in the huge bone cemetery spread out in front of them. With a dry, crackling sound, the professor's paws crushed the remains of species that major museums would have fought to have.

Then Axel picked up and held before him one of their greatest discoveries yet—a human skull! Finding a human skull this many miles below the Earth's surface was an incredible discovery.

To the professor, this skull was special. It was more than three million years old. For many years, scientists had been trying to prove that mankind existed that long ago. And right there, in front of the professor's eyes, was the proof. He gazed around and saw more specimens from that ancient era.

Once again, Professor Lidenbrock had to ask himself how these incredible specimens had ended up so many miles into the Earth's crust. Had these people fallen through the Earth to their death? Or had they survived the terrible fall into the core of the Earth and continued to live out their lives there, beneath the soil? This discovery was very similar to the mastodon bones they had seen some days ago. Could these people also be wandering the shores of this sea?

"Axel," the professor said, breaking their surprised silence, "put this specimen into your bag. My fellow scientists back in Hamburg will be amazed to see this souvenir from our journey."

Axel did as his uncle instructed. He carefully placed the skull into the specimen bag he kept slung around his neck.

"Come," the professor continued. "Let us keep searching. It seems that every discovery we make is more fantastic than the one before!"

They continued their walk along the beach. Then they saw the stone cliffs fall back to reveal a huge alcove. Climbing the sandy dunes, the professor and Axel made their way toward the giant cave. When they reached the top of a connecting dune, they saw that the professor's predictions about making more great discoveries had come true once again.

Spread out before them and reaching as far as they could see into the giant cave was an underground forest. This was not like the forest they saw earlier. It was a collection of palms, cypress, and conifers, or cone-bearing trees. All of them were connected by a twisted mass of creeping plants. A lush carpet of moss and ferns covered the ground. Trickling brooks flowed beneath the huge trees. This was one of the most unusual, spectacular sights one would expect to see so many miles beneath the Earth's surface.

As the two examined the vegetation, the professor saw many different species. All of them had three things in common.

"Axel, can you look here and find even one species of tree or shrub that has not been extinct aboveground for at least a million years?" Professor Lidenbrock asked his amazed nephew.

"I cannot say that I can," Axel replied. "Uncle, did you also notice that the vegetation is all a similar color—brownish and faded-looking—and that it has no odor to it at all?"

"Yes—interesting facts," said the professor.

The soft moss felt good and welcoming beneath Professor Lidenbrock's paws. Still, he made his way through the forest with caution. After what they had experienced in the middle of the Central Sea, this underground paradise could end up being the home of other mighty beasts, as well. He lifted his nose into the cool breeze, searching for clues. He wasn't quite sure what he was searching for. His nose was used to picking up smells on the Earth's surface. Still, he took in all the new aromas with delight and wonder.

Together, the professor and his nephew walked through what was turning out to be a huge jungle. Axel examined each of the different species and recorded information about them in a small notebook. The professor continued to make his way through the dense vegetation. His keen hearing picked up a distant noise that sounded like a tree falling. He looked over at Axel and realized his nephew had not heard the noise—he was in the middle of cataloging an ancient bush.

Professor Lidenbrock looked back to where the sound had come from. He leaped over a small brook and nosed his way through a large fern. Then he was looking out onto a large clearing. There he saw the source of the noise. He watched, in the distance, as several fourteen-foot, brown, fur-covered elephants pulled at tree leaves and low-lying bushes with their mighty trunks. "Mastodons!" the professor said to himself. "Incredible!"

He turned back to call for Axel. His nephew was already creeping toward him. Axel's eyes were wide, and his mouth was gaping open. He was speechless at the fantastic scene they were witnessing.

"Mastodons," the professor repeated. He continued in a hushed tone: "It is an entire herd of them. They are not fossils, not just a collection of bones—but living, breathing, eating mastodons!"

A tree trunk cracked loudly, then fell directly in front of them. One of the herd's members had been feeding so close to the professor and Axel's side of the clearing that they had not noticed him. The mighty creature paused no more than fifteen feet away from the travelers. Its giant sad eyes looked at both of them for any

signs of danger. After it found none, its long trunk wrapped itself around one of the fallen tree's limbs and quickly stripped it of most of its leaves. The giant beast then plunged the leaves into its mouth. It chewed with great energy. Still, the animal kept a careful watch on the two explorers.

Professor Lidenbrock slowly began to move. He wanted to get an even closer look at the ancient creature. Axel quickly placed a steadying hand on his uncle's back. The professor turned in order to see why Axel had stopped him.

Axel, eyes wide open, pointed his finger toward a huge clearing. Professor Lidenbrock followed Axel's gaze. What he saw was almost too hard for him to believe.

Not more than a quarter of a mile away, leaning against the trunk of an enormous tree, was a human being. But it wasn't just any human being. This man was an absolute giant, capable of driving and guiding the herd of huge mastodons that grazed before him. His height was over twelve feet. His head, as big as the head of a buffalo, was lost in a mane of matted hair.

"A mighty hunter, stalking one of these creatures," Axel said, his voice trembling with a touch of fear.

"No, Axel," the professor whispered. "Look at the large branch in his hand. Surely he uses such a tool to guide this mighty herd. He is a shepherd, my dear boy!"

Suddenly, the skull they had found on the ground in the bone cemetery was no longer just an old fossil. It was once a part of the body of someone who had died only recently. These people were living *here and now*. This was their time; this was their world. Now the professor and Axel were the ones out of place.

"Axel, let us leave this area," said the professor. He slowly backed farther into the forest. "We might be seen by the giant shepherd at any moment. Let the only one who knows we were here be this powerful mastodon that stands chewing before us."

Carefully, both the professor and Axel made their way back through the underground forest and to the beach.

During the walk back to the beach, the professor and Axel said nothing to each other. Professor Lidenbrock was too busy trying to make sense of the wonders they had just seen. He supposed Axel was doing the same.

It all seemed absolutely impossible! It seemed as if their ears and eyes had tricked them somehow! How could any human being have possibly existed in that underground world? But, then again, how could two ancient creatures from millions of years ago do battle with each other in the present day? There seemed to be no end to the astonishing discoveries they would make during their journey.

They returned to their raft. Hans had almost completed his repairs. As the professor and Axel approached the guide, Hans reached into a pocket and pulled out a rust-covered dagger. He turned the handle toward Axel and then offered it to him. Axel took the dagger. Hans turned his attention back to the raft.

"Is that your dagger, Axel?" the professor asked. "What made you bring along such a useless weapon?"

"I have never seen this before," Axel replied. "And I have never seen it carried by Hans, either. Are you sure it is not from your own collection?"

"Not that I know of," said the professor, puzzled. "It was never my property."

Axel kneeled, letting his uncle examine the dagger more closely. "Then what can it be?" Axel asked. "Could it be the weapon of some ancient warrior, or of some friend of that mighty shepherd from whom we have just escaped?"

Professor Lidenbrock sniffed the dagger carefully. "The rust on this weapon is not a day old, not a year old, not a century old . . . but much more!" he exclaimed. His tail began to wag as the idea struck him. The professor then backed up and looked at his nephew. "Axel," he cried, "we are now on the verge of another great discovery!" He looked back at the dagger. "This blade that Hans has discovered was left on the sand more than three hundred years ago. This dagger was a sixteenth-century weapon carried by gentlemen."

"But who brought it here?" Axel asked. "It didn't get here by itself."

"A man brought it here," the professor replied, his tail wagging much faster. "It is the same man who has probably written his name somewhere with this very dagger. It is a man who has tried once more to point the way toward the right path to the interior of the Earth!" Professor Lidenbrock took off toward the stony cliffs that lay just over the dunes. "Let us look around! You have no idea of the importance of this great discovery!"

With Axel not far behind, Professor Lidenbrock ran over the dunes and up to one of the cliff walls. Together, they searched along the wall for any sign of its previous meeting with humanity. The professor scanned the wall for any marks. He also sniffed the ground, trying to pick up any scent at all, no matter what its age was.

At last, under a huge overhanging rock, they discovered the entrance of a dark and gloomy tunnel. There, on the wall, were two letters. They were the initials of the brave and extraordinary traveler who had gone before them on their adventurous journey!

"A. S.!" Professor Lidenbrock cried. His front two paws rested just under the faded letters. "You see? I was right! Arne Saknussemm!"

The professor backed away from the wall. For a moment he was speechless. He took two quick steps and then leaped into the air, spinning his body completely around and landing on all fours.

"Wonderful and glorious genius! Great Saknussemm!" he cried with glee. "You have engraved your initials at every important stage of your journey. Your mark leads the hopeful traveler directly to the great and mighty discoveries to which you gave such energy and courage! The brave traveler shall follow your footsteps to the last. And I'm sure we will find your initials engraved, with your own hand, upon the center of the Earth itself! I will be that brave traveler—I, too, will carve my initials upon the very same spot!"

"Forward! Forward!" Axel cried, in a burst of true and strong enthusiasm. He started in the direction of the new tunnel.

"Be patient and calm, dear nephew," the professor said. It almost seemed as if their roles had become reversed. "Let us return to our good friend, Hans, and bring our supplies to this entrance."

113

They left the spot where the old initials had been carved and turned toward the beach.

"Let us leave this level sea," Professor Lidenbrock said. "We shall descend, descend, and forever continue to descend! Do you know, my dear boy, that to reach the very center of the Earth, we have only four thousand nine hundred miles left to travel?"

"Bah!" Axel cried. "The distance is scarcely worth speaking about!"

They both laughed as they traveled back to Hans and their raft. As they walked, the professor became filled with joy over the new discovery. But even the uncovering of the initials seemed to be unimportant compared to his nephew's fresh sense of courage and adventure.

The professor looked up at Axel. He saw a smile on his face, and the young man was bursting with excitement. It seemed that after coming into contact with giant mushrooms, thrashing monsters, ancient forests, great herds of mastodons, and a twelve-foot-tall human, Axel had begun to appreciate the true meaning of their expedition.

They reached Hans, gathered their supplies, and began the next part of their trek without delay. This time, Axel led the way. The three travelers climbed the sandy dunes that separated them from the new tunnel.

When they reached the entrance, Hans switched on their Ruhmkorf coil to light up the dark tunnel. Then, once again, Axel, Professor Lidenbrock, and Hans stepped inside a dark tunnel, heading ever closer toward the center of the Earth!

They began to follow the passageway in a straight direction. Then, after taking about twelve steps forward, they had to stop. An enormous granite boulder blocked the entire tunnel. The travelers peered to the left and right for another passage, but there was none. They looked above and below the mighty boulder for any kind of opening. Again, there was none.

"Oh, this miserable stone!" Axel said angrily, pounding on the huge rock.

Professor Lidenbrock walked anxiously back and forth in front of the giant granite barricade. Hans simply seated himself calmly on a rock, the kind he always seemed able to find.

"What about Arne Saknussemm?" Axel asked his uncle.

This remark pulled the professor out of his silent thoughts. "You are right," he replied. "He would never have been stopped by a lump of rock!"

"No—ten thousand times no!" Axel replied with great determination. "This lump of rock is the result of some underground earthquake that happened long after Saknussemm passed through here. He never met this challenge. If we do not overcome it, then we are

unworthy of following in the footsteps of the great explorer. We will be unable to find our way to the center of the Earth!"

Professor Lidenbrock's enthusiasm was renewed by his nephew's wise words. "Well," he said, his tail wagging wildly, "let us go to work with pickaxes, with crowbars, with anything that we can get our hands on!"

"The rock is far too solid and too big to be destroyed by a pickaxe or crowbar," Axel replied.

"What, then?" the professor asked.

"No ordinary tools can be used on such a rock," Axel said. "What we need is gunpowder!"

"Yes!" Professor Lidenbrock cried. "We must get rid of this stumbling block!" He turned to Hans. "To work, Hans, to work!"

Their guide slid his pack off his back. He opened it and pulled out a huge crowbar. With that, he began to dig a hole under the rock. It was a difficult task. It had to be done, though. Hans dug a hole large enough to hold fifty pounds of powerful gun cotton—a substance four times as powerful as ordinary gunpowder.

While Hans worked, the professor watched Axel pour a long trail of gunpowder out of the tunnel and along the granite wall. This gunpowder would be their fuse. When Hans was finished, Axel placed the explosive gun cotton into the hole.

Everything was in place. The three eager adventurers prepared to continue their journey. Professor Lidenbrock and Hans left the tunnel and took their place upon the raft. Axel followed them out. Then he prepared to light the long fuse he had poured onto the cavern's floor.

From the raft, the professor and Hans watched Axel. He struck a match across the granite wall, then touched it to the end of the line of gunpowder. There was an immediate flash as the powder ignited. A long column of smoke rose into the air from the tiny bright flame that danced along the black trail of powder leading into the tunnel.

Axel ran quickly to the shore and hopped onto the waiting raft. Once he was on board, Hans hoisted the sail in order to get as far away from the explosion as possible to safely avoid the falling rock. When the professor believed they had sailed far enough away from the shore to be safe, he told Hans to lower the sail. Once the sail was down, each of them waited impatiently for the coming blast.

"Now, then," the professor cried, "mountains of granite crumble beneath the power of man!"

Wow! Thrashing monsters, herds of mastodons, and a giant caveman! I didn't know all of that stuff was under the surface of the Earth! I'd better remember not to bury my toys too deep. I don't want any mastodons reaching up and chewing on my squeaky book!

Chapter Eleven

Wishbone stepped outside through the opened front door. He saw a tired Wanda Gilmore sitting by the edge of the hole in their front yard. Awkwardly holding the shovel close to the blade, she lifted it out of the hole with just a tiny bit of dirt on it. She dumped the dirt near, but not on top of, the neat pile the kids had made earlier. It was clear Wanda was exhausted and didn't have the strength that an experienced digger like Wishbone had. *The key is plenty of practice, Wanda—plenty of practice.*

Wishbone watched his tired neighbor. At the same time, Joe, David, Sam, and Ellen rushed past him and made their way toward Wanda and the hole. Not wanting to be left out of the action, Wishbone quickly followed.

Ellen kneeled next to Wanda. Each of the kids grabbed a nearby shovel and began to dig furiously. Dirt flew as the kids attacked the hole from all sides, making it deeper and wider.

"Well, finally you decide to come back," Wanda said in a tired tone.

None of the kids responded, however. They continued to hack away at the hole.

"Now, *that's* what I call digging!" Wanda said, as she

watched the kids put all their strength into the task at hand.

"Power digging!" Wishbone said with a bark. The smell of the fresh soil was getting him excited.

Each of the kids continued to remove shovelful after shovelful of dirt from the ever-growing hole.

"Hey, kids," Wanda said with concern, "I'd say that's good enough."

Focused on their task, none of the kids responded.

"I mean," Wanda continued, "I think that hole is deep enough."

Neither Joe, Sam, nor David moved their eyes away from the hole. As if the kids were all experienced construction workers, they removed a shovel load of dirt one at a time. Each one stepped back to empty it, letting the next one plunge the shovel into the hole.

"Kids, please stop!" Wanda cried.

Ellen put a comforting hand on Wanda's shoulder. "Wanda, it's okay," she told her friend. "They're just trying to find something."

"Please don't worry, Wanda," Wishbone added. "Haven't you ever dug for buried treasure before?"

Interested, Wanda leaned over the hole, as if hoping

to catch a glimpse at what the kids were looking for. Sam pulled a load of dirt out of the hole and dumped it onto the growing pile. Joe stepped up his pace and drove his shovel deep into the hole. When it reached the bottom, it hit with a loud *clink!*

"Uh-oh," Wishbone said, backing up. "This can't be good."

Suddenly, a wide, powerful stream of water shot out of the hole and sprayed directly into Wanda's face.

"Turn it off! Turn it off!" Wanda cried, trying to block the gushing water with her hands. "Somebody turn it off!"

Ellen and the kids couldn't help laughing as Wanda fought against the miniature geyser.

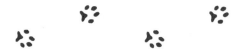

Hey, that stream of water shooting up from the ground reminds me of something. . . .

Oh, right! I almost forgot! The professor and his crew are floating on their raft as they wait for their gunpowder charge to explode. Little do they know that they will soon see another geyser of their own!

Chapter Twelve

*B*oom!!!
The roar of the blast was incredible. The deafening sound echoed through the cavern and out into the sea. Pieces of stone shot out of the blocked tunnel and over the sea as if a giant cannon were firing at threatening ships.

Luckily, the raft was a safe distance away from the blast. Most of the larger bits of stone landed in the sea in front of it. Yet, tiny pieces still showered over the raft as the water it floated upon rippled from the vibrations sent throughout the giant cavern.

Once the explosion had ended, Professor Lidenbrock removed his paws from over his ears. Then, as the echo from the blast faded, the professor, Axel, and Hans stared back at the part of the shore that was now marked by a smoky cloud of dust.

"Hans," the professor said suddenly, "let us return to land and see if our work has been a success." Hans quickly paddled the raft toward the sandy beach.

The Icelander rowed a few strokes. Then he stopped and tilted his head to one side, as if listening for something. Seeing this, the professor did the same, but all he heard was the fading echo of the explosion. . . .

Wait a minute—is the echo really fading? the professor thought. As he listened, it seemed to remain strangely at the same level, which was completely wrong. From what they had experienced of the vastness of this sea and the cavern in which it lay, the rumbling echo should have faded. But it hadn't. In fact, it now seemed a bit louder!

A small splash near the raft pulled the professor from his thoughts. He looked around to see pieces of stone fall from the clouds above and land in the sea around them. The professor then looked toward the shore. There he saw stones break loose from the cavern walls and smash into the ground below. Large sprays of sand flew into the air when the stones hit the ground.

"It would seem that we have triggered off something other than the boulder with our explosion!" the professor yelled over the even louder rumble. "It seems we have interrupted something that would have probably been best left undisturbed!"

The constant thunder became louder than ever. The seawater sloshed back and forth from the vibration. The waves splashed over the sides of the raft as it was tossed by the sudden vibrating storm.

An ear-splitting crack drew the professor's attention upward. It sounded as if the entire ceiling of the giant cavern was about to come crashing down upon them. But all that Lidenbrock could see was electricity dancing through a cloudy haze.

Without warning, a giant stone ten times the size of the raft fell from the clouds. The blue lightning danced across the huge rock's surface as it ripped through the cloudy haze. The threatening object was enormous, and it was plunging directly in the path of the flimsy raft.

"Hans!" the professor yelled.

The Icelander looked up. Without a moment of delay, he frantically began to paddle the endangered raft.

Axel, upon following the professor's gaze, shoved his arm into the water and began to paddle, as well.

Axel and Hans's desperate paddling saved the raft and its passengers from a deadly fate. When the giant stone slammed into the water's surface, it plunged only inches away from the raft's edge. Its first impact almost overturned the craft and its three crewmen. As the stone sank, the force from the suction almost pulled the raft down with it.

When the sea had calmed from the giant rock's splash, Professor Lidenbrock looked up to where it had fallen from. As he suspected, he saw the clouds being sucked into the huge hole in the cavern's ceiling where the stone had once sat. It seemed as if they had poked a hole in the sky.

Suddenly, the raft heaved beneath them with a great force. The professor had to use the nails on all four paws just to cling to the raft's surface. Most of their supplies were hurled over the side as the raft shot upward. Hans and Axel held on for dear life, as well.

"Another sea monster!" Axel cried with terror.

"No!" the professor yelled above the now deafening roar. "This monster is a geyser—a giant surge of water pushing up from the sea floor. No doubt we set off a volcanic reaction with our explosion!" He looked back to the enormous hole in the cavern's ceiling. It was getting closer as the geyser pushed them upward toward it.

"Volcanic?" Axel cried, his arms wrapped tightly around the mast.

The raft hurled toward the cavern's ceiling and toward the huge hole that had been carved out of it. Electricity flickered all around them as they passed through the illuminating clouds. The professor looked up into the hole. He realized that it was the beginning of a long tunnel leading upward as far as he could see. Then the three travelers were thrust into darkness as the field of electricity was left behind them.

Through the roar of the rushing water below them, Professor Lidenbrock heard the striking of a match and the spark of fire as Hans tried to light a lantern. Their Rumhkorf coil had gone over the side of the raft with the rest of their gear. Luckily, though, Hans had been able to save one of their regular lanterns.

Once the lantern was lit, the shaft they were hurling through was illuminated with a dim, warm glow. The shaft was about three times as wide as the raft. The raft itself bobbed on a cushion of churning water. All around them, solid rock whizzed past them at incredible speeds.

"Not only have we set off a volcanic reaction," the professor said, "but we seem to be right inside a volcano."

"*Inside* a volcano?" Axel asked in surprise. "Uncle, are you sure?"

"Most definitely," Professor Lidenbrock said. "Do you not already notice the rapid rise in temperature?"

"I think I am too frightened to tell," Axel replied.

The professor walked over to an edge of the wobbling, but more stable, raft. "Then look here," he said to his nephew. "Do you not see the steam beginning to rise?" The professor placed his paw next to the edge where a small billowing cloud of steam had begun to emerge. "If my calculations are correct, a large body of lava is pushing the mass of water on which we ride to the surface. A most fortunate thing!"

"Fortunate?" Axel cried. He seemed not to believe what he was hearing.

"Yes, dear nephew," the professor replied calmly. "It is the only chance we now have to escape from the interior of the Earth and go back into the true light of day." He turned to Hans, then looked back to Axel. "If we cannot continue on Saknussemm's trail, then this is our best hope."

"You speak of hope," Axel said. "But how is there hope in being spit out of the Earth with showers of cinders and boiling lava?"

"While there is life, there is hope," Professor Lidenbrock replied. "I wish to tell you something most important, Axel. As long as a man's heart beats, as long as a man can have feelings, as long as a dog's tail wags, and as long as people are blessed with thought and determination, there is no room for despair!"

Axel and Hans stared at the professor in silence.

Professor Lidenbrock trotted over to where Axel was sitting. "I do believe the situation is, to a certain extent, desperate." He placed a comforting paw on Axel's arm. "There remains, however, a good chance of survival," the professor continued. "We must prepare ourselves for whatever may turn up in the great chapter of accidents."

"But will the lava not eventually make its way to the raft itself?" Axel asked. He was still clinging to the mast.

"It could very well happen, indeed," Professor Lidenbrock replied. "However, the logs, which were so carefully chosen by Hans, should protect us from the lava for a short time." *I just hope it will be long enough,* the professor thought to himself.

The raft continued to hurl upward through the throat of the volcano. The professor's nose dripped with sweat as the temperature continued to rise as fast as the raft did. It seemed as if the heat was not coming from just below them, but from all around, as if the entire Earth were made of fire.

Their rapid climb made it difficult to breathe, and Professor Lidenbrock panted to catch his breath. He looked around and saw that both Axel and Hans were dripping with sweat, as well.

As the professor watched his fellow travelers, however, he noticed he could see them more clearly. A quick look upward confirmed what he believed. At the top of the long tunnel, there was a small dot of bright light—a dot that was growing in size by the second.

"Axel! Hans!" the professor shouted. "Look! Do you see? We are nearing the top of the volcano!"

What had taken them almost a month to travel away from was now approaching quickly due to their incredible speed. The daylight that shone through the volcano's mouth was getting brighter and brighter.

The professor's head spun as he tried to calculate the speed at which they traveled. They had been almost a hundred miles below the Earth's surface. Now the light from the volcano's mouth approached them like the light of a speeding locomotive!

The raft tipped and turned as it gained even more speed. With the opening of the volcano getting closer, the bright light of day was almost blinding to someone who had been underground for such a long period of time. Smoke was beginning to rise as the liquid, fiery lava made its way to the underside of the raft.

"Hold on, my friends!" the professor yelled. He moved closer to the center of the raft, where Axel and Hans were clinging desperately. He gave a reassuring lick to Axel's hand just before they were all swallowed up inside a blinding light!

Professor Lidenbrock slowly awoke to find himself in Hans's arms. He was being placed next to a semiconscious Axel. The air was full of smoke and the scent of what smelled like burning coal. Trying to identify his surroundings, the professor looked around groggily. Through squinting eyes, he saw they were sitting on the slope of a mountain not two yards from a huge cliff. They would have fallen from it if they made the slightest false step.

"Where are we?" moaned the professor.

Hans just shrugged his shoulders.

When his eyes had fully adjusted to the warm sunlight, the professor gazed at the mysterious landscape. Above them, he saw the opened crater from which they had escaped. It continued to spit fire and cinders into the air. From where they were perched, however, they were safe from its eruptions—at least for now. The professor's eyes followed the slope of the giant volcano downward to see it disappear into a lush green forest.

The professor then saw the waters of what was either a lovely sea or beautiful lake. He gazed even farther. He saw a little port, crowded with houses. Nearby, boats and vessels of a strange shape were floating upon turquoise waves.

"Where can we be?" Axel asked, looking at the same setting.

The professor stood on four wobbly legs. "Whatever this mountain may be," he said, "I do not think it is worthwhile to have left the interior of a volcano and remain here to receive huge pieces of rock on our heads." He turned to face the base of the volcano. "Let us carefully go down the mountain and discover where we are." *And maybe we'll have a nice snack,* he thought. *Being blasted out of a volcano can really work up your appetite!*

The three explorers slowly made their way down the steep, slippery slope. They slid over piles of ash, trying desperately to avoid the streams of hot lava that flowed like fiery serpents.

When they reached the bottom of the volcano, Professor Lidenbrock led the way to a spring of fresh water that fed a small brook. The professor bent his head forward and lapped up the cool water. On each side of him he heard Axel and Hans do the same. *What a sight we must be,* he thought. *Three tired travelers, most of our clothes either ripped or burned, all of us lined up in a row, on our bellies, drinking from a stream.* Professor Lidenbrock let out a small chuckle in between swallows.

The professor raised his head. In front of him, between two olive trees, a small child stood, watching the very strange sight he had just had in his thoughts.

"Ah," he said, "here's someone who lives in this country."

The little boy was poorly dressed. As soon as he realized he had been seen, he began to run away. Hans quickly jumped over the stream and took hold of the boy, despite his kicks and cries. The professor and Axel joined the two.

"What is the name of this mountain?" the professor asked the frightened youth. The child made no reply. Professor Lidenbrock went on to ask him the same question in English and French. Still, the boy said nothing. When the professor asked the same question in Italian, the boy yelled, "Stromboli!" Then he dashed away from Hans's grasp and disappeared into the olive groves.

"Stromboli!" the professor repeated with amazement. "What a journey! What a marvelous journey!" Professor Lidenbrock leaped into the air with glee and laughed.

"Is it what I think it is, Uncle?" Axel asked, as if he didn't want to get his hopes up.

"Yes, dear nephew," the professor replied. "We entered the Earth by way of one volcano in the gray, icy regions of Iceland, and we have come out of another one under the blue sky of the island of Sicily, just off the coast of Italy. We are more than two thousand miles away from where we started!"

When Hans heard the name "Stromboli," he, too, laughed with amazement. It was the most emotion he'd shown throughout the entire journey. Axel and the professor looked at each other and smiled. Professor Lidenbrock supposed that Hans could not believe how far their adventure had taken them. What an incredible journey!

The three explorers enjoyed a delicious meal of olives, fruits, and fresh water. Then they began the end of their incredible journey as they made their way to the port of Stromboli. In order not to be mistaken by the locals as spirits that had been shot out of the volcano, Professor Lidenbrock decided they would pretend to be unfortunate shipwrecked travelers.

As they walked through the forest in the direction of the port, Axel let Hans take the lead. He fell back to walk with his uncle. "Thank you, Uncle," he said softly.

"'Thank you'?" the professor asked, his tail wagging slightly. "Why, what ever for, dear boy?"

"Thank you for showing me the incredible wonders we have seen," Axel replied. "Thank you for showing me my strength, my courage. But, most of all, thank you for taking me with you on this fantastic journey." Professor Lidenbrock's tail wagged harder now. Axel continued: "I'm proud to be the nephew of the great Professor Lidenbrock, member of all the scientific, geographical, mineralogical, and geological societies."

The professor stopped walking. So did Axel. The professor placed his two front paws on Axel's legs. "My dear nephew," Professor Lidenbrock began, "you honor me with your kind words. We have been on a most incredible journey. We have made many very important discoveries. We have also seen things that perhaps no one will even believe. We have been on the edge of death and back, as well as having traveled to the depths of the Earth." He looked to the now distant volcano, then back at Axel. "But of one thing I am certain with

all my heart—I couldn't have done any of it without you, Axel."

Axel rubbed a hand across his uncle's head. "Thank you, Uncle."

"No, Axel," the professor said, "*I* thank *you*." The professor got back down on the ground and continued through the forest toward Hans. With his tail still wagging, he began to run. He looked back to see that Axel was doing the same.

"Come, dear boy!" he yelled back at his adventurous nephew. "The whole world waits to hear of our discoveries. Everyone wishes to see the three explorers who have been on a most incredible journey toward the center of the Earth!"

What a great adventure! A trip to Iceland, climbing into a volcano, sailing across an underground sea, and being spat out of an active volcano! I'll say one thing about Professor Lidenbrock—*he* really knows how to cure a case of boredom.

Now it's time to see where our adventure in Oakdale is going to end up!

Chapter Thirteen

Wishbone watched as Wanda tried to fight off the stream of water that was shooting directly into her face from the hole in the Talbots' yard. He started to wag his tail, but he stopped before anyone saw. This definitely was not funny . . . well, not much.

"Turn the water off!" Wanda gurgled with a mouthful of water. "Someone turn it off!"

Wishbone heard a squeak near the house. He turned to see Joe kneeling next to the house. With his arm, he reached inside a hole. In his other hand, he held up a green-plastic lid that was made for the hole. The squeak seemed to come from whatever he was turning. Wishbone turned back toward Wanda to see the stream of water slowly die down. *So that's what that hole was for over there,* Wishbone thought. *I'll have to remember that.*

Dripping wet, Wanda stood up. "I tried to tell you!" she said. "You dug too deep and hit your sprinkler line!"

Ellen Talbot, who was still laughing, got to her feet and put an arm around Wanda. "Wanda, I'm so sorry," she said, trying to control her laughter.

All human eyes were on Wanda. Wishbone's eyes were on the hole—or, what was *in* the hole. As he walked over and peered down, a glint of gold in the bottom of the hole caught his attention. "I see ya!" he yelled. He dove, headfirst, into the hole.

The hole was so deep now, Wishbone could easily fit his whole body into it. *Hey,* Wishbone thought, *I could put my entire squeaky collection in a hole like this!* With his nails, he scraped some of the dirt off the gold piece he saw. Then he grabbed it firmly in his teeth and headed out.

"Well, you see, Miss Gilmore," Wishbone heard Joe say, "there was this medal that we found . . ."

"I got it!" Wishbone yelled between clenched teeth as he came out of the hole. He brought his find up to Joe.

"Wait a minute," Joe said curiously. "What is that, Wishbone?"

Wishbone spat out the object into Joe's hand. "Bleh!" Wishbone's tongue kept slurping out of his mouth. "Bleh! Bleh! There's some dirt stuck between my teeth. Bleh!"

"It can't be!" Joe exclaimed, as he examined the piece.

Sam moved closer to Joe to get a better look. "It's the other piece of the medal!"

Joe patted Wishbone on the head. "Way to go, Wishbone!"

Wishbone circled around proudly. "Thank you. It was nothing."

Joe gave the second piece to his mom. Then she placed the two pieces together and began to translate the inscription on the second piece. "'Outstanding courage, awarded this day, May 5, 1864, to Noah Johnstone.'"

"N. J.!" Joe, Sam, and David said all together.

"So he's the culprit!" Wishbone said with a bark.

Wanda blinked. Then she looked at Ellen and the medal in her hand. "Did you say Noah Johnstone?" she asked excitedly. "*Colonel* Noah Johnstone?"

Everyone looked at one another in confusion. Ellen looked at the medal again, as if she were trying to remember reading the name "Colonel."

"Colonel?" Sam said. "So he was in the Civil War!"

David stepped forward. "Yes, Miss Gilmore," he added. "We found a picture of the medal in a book on the Civil War that we borrowed from the library." He pointed to the medal. "It said hardly anything about it, though— just that the medal was a limited issue, not given to many people."

Now it was Joe's turn. "And it said something else." He tried hard to think. "U. S. . . . ."

"USCT?" Wanda asked knowingly.

"Yes!" Sam exclaimed. "That was it!"

Wanda smiled. "Well, kids, I'm sure you would have found out once you researched the matter more. But 'USCT' stands for 'United States Colored Troops.'" Everyone looked at one another in silence as Wanda continued. "At first, African-Americans weren't allowed to fight at all in the Civil War. Then, after President Abraham Lincoln

135

issued the Emancipation Proclamation, which freed all slaves, the USCT was formed."

"The men helped fight for their own freedom," David added excitedly.

"Absolutely right, David," Wanda said with a smile. "Former slaves—as well as freemen from the North—joined the United States Colored Troops. Unfortunately, there weren't as many records kept on the USCT as there were for other troops. But there were a lot of heroes in those troops."

"Like Noah Johnstone," Joe said.

"That's right." Wanda was more excited now. "In fact, Colonel Johnstone helped save his entire regiment when he noticed Confederates sneaking up on them as they were building a bridge. . . . And this is *his* medal?" Wanda continued.

She took the medal from Ellen and held it carefully. She looked at Ellen and the kids.

   ·   "I can't believe I'm really holding this," Wanda said. She gazed at the medal again. "This medal had been lost for years." Wanda paused for a moment. "Until now."

"How do you know so much about this guy?" Joe asked.

"This guy," Wanda replied with surprise, "was the very first mayor of the town we all live in!" Wanda walked over to the wheelbarrow and placed a hand on the small oak tree. "Why, tradition has it that Noah Johnstone planted many of the original oak trees in Oakdale!" Wanda looked around at all her friends' faces. "Thank you," she said, her eyes glistening with tears. "Thank you so much for finding this." Wanda rubbed a thumb over the medal's inscription. "I would love to add this to our collection at the Oakdale Historical Society." She looked back at the kids. "Well, I mean, if it's okay with you."

Smiling, everyone looked at one another, then back

at Wanda. Then came loud shouts of "Sure! . . . Great! . . . Absolutely!"

Wanda looked down at Wishbone. "What do you think, Wishbone?"

Wishbone dove headfirst into the hole. "No time for chitchat, Wanda!" he said as he crawled to the bottom and began to dig with all his energy.

"Wishbone?" he heard Wanda call from above him, but he kept going.

"I've got new treasure to find, new lands to explore!" He was in full digging mode. "Onward—to the center of the Earth!"

About Jules Verne

Jules Verne, who some say was the father of science fiction, was born on February 8, 1828, in Nantes, France. Although Verne studied law, his real passion was for the theater and literature.

In 1850, Verne's first play was produced. In 1863, Verne published his first story of an adventure journey, *Five Weeks in a Balloon*. He was inspired to write the novel after he heard of a scientist who planned to take a journey in a box held up by a huge balloon. So, *Five Weeks in a Balloon* was fiction based on scientific fact—science fiction!

Verne went on to write and publish many other science fiction stories, including *A Journey to the Center of the Earth, From Earth to the Moon, Twenty Thousand Leagues Under the Sea,* and *The Mysterious Island.* In each book, Verne continued to stretch the boundaries of science to create amazing, yet believable, tales of adventure and discovery.

In all of his wonderful literary journeys, Verne's insight accurately described many inventions that were unheard of in his day, but are quite common today. They include: the electric lamp, the submarine, and space travel. Not only have Verne's works inspired inventions and ideas, but his books have also been the basis for many movies and television shows.

With themes that easily translate to our day and age, Verne's stories, ideas, and concepts continue to delight and inspire writers of all ages around the world.

About *A Journey to the Center of the Earth*

A Journey to the Center of the Earth was written by Jules Verne in 1864. The story is presented from Axel's point of view and expresses his fears about traveling deep into the Earth's core. This science fiction classic also explores Axel's concern over what he thinks is his uncle's obsession, his joy of discovery, and his newfound courage to complete the journey. The book is written to seem more like a journal, rather than a novel, with notes on all the discoveries, as well as many of the scientific theories of the time.

As with many of Verne's books, quite a few of the ideas portrayed in *A Journey to the Center of the Earth* were based on scientific facts. The Ruhmkorf coils were based on early theories about electricity. Verne basically predicted a primitive version of a flashlight. The mastodons, the plesiosaurus, and the ichthyosaurus were all real creatures, and they did exist in prehistoric times. Scientists today assume that these animals are extinct and don't exist deep beneath the surface of the Earth. But, then again, could such creatures still roam around in Earth's deepest hidden places? After all, how many people have traveled as deep into the Earth as Professor Lidenbrock?

After reading *Digging to the Center of the Earth*, you'll note that Professor Lidenbrock, his nephew, Axel, and their trusty guide, Hans, never reached the actual center of the Earth. Nor did Professor Lidenbrock get to carve his initials next to those of the famed Arne Saknussemm. Professor Lidenbrock was certain that the great explorer had carved his initials into the Earth's very center itself. This is also true of the original novel.

The premature ending of the three travelers' journey leaves plenty of room for readers to use their imagination and to wonder what else might have happened. While on their journey, Professor Lidenbrock and his companions had found living dinosaurs, mastodons, and a giant caveman. Think of what wonders they would have discovered if they had continued deeper into the Earth!

You can, however, complete their journey for them. Remember, there's no limit to the incredible discoveries your imagination can create. Even more exciting finds could be waiting for the next adventurous travelers who dare to go on their own journey to the center of the Earth!

About Michael Anthony Steele

Michael Anthony Steele—or Ant, as he is known to his friends—first worked on the crew of the WISHBONE television show as a prop assistant during the filming of the show's first season. In fact, during the production of *Hot Diggety Dawg*, the episode that was based on *A Journey to the Center of the Earth*, Ant actually carved Arne Saknussemm's initials into the rock wall. Of course, it didn't take Ant as long as it might have taken Saknussemm to carve his initials. This rock wall was made only of Styrofoam.

During the second season of the television show, Ant worked as a staff writer. He had the chance to co-write the one-hour Halloween special, *Halloween Hound: The Legend of Creepy Collars*; the TV episode *War of the Noses*; and Wishbone's movie, *WISHBONE's Dog Days of the West*.

Ant's other writing credits include the WISHBONE Mysteries *Forgotten Heroes* and the script for the CD-ROM *Wishbone Activity Zone*.

Ant has always been a fan of Jules Verne's works, and of science fiction in general. He also has a good background for writing for a dog, because he has rarely lived in a household that didn't have a canine in it.

While writing *Digging to the Center of the Earth*, Ant made good use of his experience with dogs. He remembered back to the farm where he grew up, and he thought about his hound dog, Duke. Duke and the family dachshund, Gretchen, used to go out into the pasture and dig holes, searching for gophers. Sometimes they would dig so deep that if Ant went looking for them, he would see only two tails sticking out of the ground.

Currently, Ant lives in Texas with his wife, Becky, and a house full of animals. They have two Chihuahuas, Juno and Echo; a Staffordshire terrier, Odessa; and an English bulldog, Rufus. Ant and Becky also have two Siamese cats, Pluto and Bromius; a snake, Bishop; and an aviary full of finches and canaries. You could say they both *really* like animals.